Nothing
to Declare

Nothing
to Declare

Richard M. Ravin

16 doors press

First paperback edition 2021

Book design by Bonnie Mettler
Author photo by Carol Baum

Library of Congress Control Number: 2020918204

ISBN 978-0-578-72296-2 (paperback)
ISBN 978-0-578-72297-9 (ebook)

www.richardmravin.com

Printed in the United States of America

For Daniel

When a man thinketh on any thing whatsoever, His next
Thought after, is not altogether so casuall as it seems to be.
—Thomas Hobbes, *Leviathan*

Dead men are heavier than broken hearts.
—Raymond Chandler, *The Big Sleep*

ONE

1990

H E'D PROMISED TO GET THERE BEFORE DARK. Mrs. Folari wasn't comfortable opening her door to strangers, not in February—the month was devoted to bad luck. But Jesse was lost and he was losing the light. His knuckles gripped the wheel more tightly with each passing block. At the smallest tap of his foot, the rented Lincoln surged forward. The thing knew where it wanted to go, even if he hadn't a clue.

He watched for street signs out of the corner of his eye. He could be anywhere, Everett, maybe, or Medford, some-place on the edge of what he remembered. Maybe he'd crossed in and out of Somerville already, its expressways and rotaries named after Korean War dead, the tiny red, white, and blue memorial flags. He couldn't tell; L.A. and its grid, its easts and wests, had bled every curve from memory.

At a blinking red light he paused and scratched at the ice on the inside of the side window: empty, windblown sidewalks and a magazine stand shilling the lottery, a muffler shop on the corner, a street sign so covered with snow he could read only the last three letters, LEY ST. Seventy-five degrees when he'd left Santa Monica this morning and the acacias in full blossom. The lanes of the Palisades had been carpeted in yellow.

The street lights popped on and lit a row of dun-colored houses with stained cars in their drives. In the middle of the block, a man dragged his garbage can to the street and propped it against a heap of snow and gravel. Before he reached his door, a gust blew the can over and spilled chicken bones and Sunday supplements. The man pivoted, the wind ballooning his overcoat, his mittened hands balled into fists. Another pivot and he stomped inside his house. The Christmas lights on his door flashed on.

Somerville, Jesse was sure of it. Marty had come back here to live, had been here for the last fourteen years, if that could be believed. Marty had hated the place, hell, they'd hated it together. Jesse steered the Lincoln carefully around the corner; a boat this big, no point chancing a ding. LEY meant DOOLEY, he hoped. The street where Marty lived. Had lived.

The phone had surprised him at 4:30 in the morning two nights before, a stranger's voice drilling into his sleep. A landlady, Mrs. Folari, her teary news delivered with broad, Boston A's and no respect for time zones. Marty had died. There'd been an accident in New Hampshire; he'd hit a deer. He'd been drinking, she whispered. Yes, Jesse'd said, thinking—of course. The landlady repeated herself. Marty was gone and Jesse was wanted.

Number fifteen was a shingled three-decker, indistinguishable from the ones on either side. The car balked as Jesse parked in front, the snow groaning under the tires, but he didn't shut off the engine until the Lincoln was parallel. The doorbell he chose had a mourning ribbon draped over a green holly wreath, the faded black satin showing good service. In this neighborhood, mourning was seldom out of season. Marty Balakian, it was his turn tonight. Jesse announced his name to the sliver of a cracked-open door.

The landlady welcomed him in and sat Jesse on her chintz settee, pressing on him cold cuts, pickled vegetables, and homemade anisette. She was just under five feet tall with a heavy sweater over her black dress, in her eighties, he guessed, and she performed her duties well-rehearsed by experience, almost gleeful to have someone to share her trouble with. On the wall behind her, a gilt-framed Jesus presided over the Folari living room.

"Mr. Kerf. Please. Take as much as you want; I made the pepperoncini special. He was a good boy."

For a moment, it wasn't clear what the woman meant. "You're talking about Marty," Jesse said.

The landlady's pupils swam behind the round lenses of her glasses. "Naturally, Mr. Balakian. My son was worried—an Armenian. He had a good face, I always go by that, and he paid on the dot every month. He shoveled the walk, you understand. A good boy, like I said." The landlady took up some knitting and watched Jesse poke at his antipasto.

A good boy—boy of fifty-two, strung out on booze and probably two or three other things, if Marty had kept to character. A good boy was hardly how he would want it.

"I'm still confused why it was me you called," Jesse said. "I haven't been in contact with Marty for longer than I like to remember. Since the time we were living in California."

"California. I've seen it in the pictures. Now I listen to the television. They have it too, the palm trees and everything. Your friend, to go so young, no children, no wife, no nothing, a waste. But he made you next of kin, the lawyer told me. I say, okay, let me take care of the telephone. You don't want bad news from a lawyer." She rummaged in her pocket, showed him a business card. "Mr. Lieb. Like you. Jewish."

Jesse took the card, touched the embossed printing with his fingertip. Mrs. Folari's mouth tensed with expectation. It was Jesse's turn now, and she was hoping for what—questions, reminiscences, the common territory of the bereaved? He thought of one of the last times he'd seen his friend, Marty in his black denim jacket and jeans and the cowboy boots he was never without. He was smoking reefer and peeling artichokes while wearing headphones that played a wild arpeggio by Ornette Coleman, the stereo cable trailing from kitchen to living room. As he trimmed and cut and rubbed with lemon, Marty did a shuffling dance step where he stood, and sang a kind of harmony in his lovely high tenor.

Mrs. Folari was waiting and Jesse felt compelled to offer something. "Marty was happy here, I take it?"

The landlady looked surprised. "Mr. Kerf. As far as I know, only the cows are happy."

Jesse took up his plate and considered the specks of fat in a slice of mortadella. "He was happy in California," he said.

The upstairs apartment was unlit, and the landing fixture brightened an uninviting sweep of vestibule Jesse hesitated to cross. From down below rose the sound of laughter, TV laughter in love with itself, the sound manufactured, no doubt, not far from where he lived. A pile of yellowed newspapers blocked the threshold. Jesse stepped over them and closed the door behind him.

His vision refused to adjust to the darkness—nothing, an exuberant blackness, the hiss of the radiators. The room was busy with odors: damp paper and, from farther away, cooking grease and smoke. The strongest layer was of sweat. This was instructive. Marty's stink had outlived him.

When Jesse found the lights, the brightness startled him, a blast of halogen from a long ceiling track. The taste of anisette came slick against his teeth. He hadn't prepared himself for what he'd find.

The living room was similar to Mrs. Folari's in size, but the comparison ended there. It contained a collection of books and nothing else. *Collection* wasn't the right word, though. There were too many to count, too many for anyone to read, the metal bookcases arranged like overstuffed library stacks. The aisles ran wall to wall, shelves of black enamel, gunmetal gray, and army green, the colors of industry. The room was empty otherwise, no furniture, no carpet over the painted floor, the plaster walls blank but for the glossy dome of a thermostat and the imprints of whatever pictures had once passed for decoration.

Jesse's eye flew across the book jackets, the spill of lettering, the shiny paper covers: American history, psychology, film studies, earth science, biography, feminist theory. Marty's imagination and interest had neglected nothing. Six banks of shelving supported eight levels each, and each of these ran the full length of the room, twelve feet or more. The metal bowed at the center from the weight. The man's canon had not changed: what's good in moderation is better in excess.

A large volume on the nearest bottom shelf displayed pages of blaring color, the human anatomy, male—standing, sitting, anterior, and posterior views. In one illustration, the corded muscles were exposed and the veins and arteries branched in a dreadful tangle. Its palms-outward posture echoed Mrs. Folari's Jesus—except for the arrogant rictus smile. We are all sinners here.

A memory surfaced of an evening when Jesse was 19. Johnny's Foodmaster on North Beacon, was it there still? Dog days, early September 1972, it would have to be. Jesse's legs shake, the dollar in his hand shakes, his bell bottoms tremble against his shins; surely the clerk can hear. A jar of capers travels down the rubber belt. Through a slit in his shirt pocket—a guayabera worn expressly for this—Jesse clutches against his belly fifteen dollars' worth of veal. The cool cellophane of the package sticks to his skin, conveys a vigorous sense of wrong. On the other side of the automatic doors, Marty's Volvo runs in the parking lot, the red eye of a cigarillo hot behind the windshield.

"Mark this, Little Brother," Marty says later, while he sprinkles lemon zest on the smoking veal. "The best ingredients, you can't buy them, they're not for sale. Look at the pan, you see veal and capers, a hit of lemon—that's base metal. They're nothing, they're meaningless. But fear and greed—stir in the big emotions and you get a dish that stands for something."

Jesse waits at the ready, pours vermouth in the pan at Marty's nod. "You see dinner," Marty says, tasting from the skillet with a hairy thumb. "I see fucking transcendence."

Jesse walked to where he'd set down his coat. The sleeves of his sweater had picked up a patina of dust, and he brushed himself off before he put it on. A week at least, he thought, to box the books, sell them, or give them away. Perhaps he would hire the work out. Who could he hire, though, to explain what had delivered Marty to his current—and final—obsession?

Jesse sighted down the hall toward the bedroom and, beyond it, the kitchen. No. He'd come in daylight; it would be easier in the light, it would have to be. As he left, Jesse lowered the temperature to sixty-two. The radiator hiss cut off and silence followed him out the door.

Snow had fallen, thick, sudden flakes that covered his car. He moved the Lincoln into traffic, feeling the engine through the sole of his shoe. What was it for skids, steer with or against? On the McGrath-O'Brien, a line of plows slanted along the roadway. They rolled at a decorous pace and left a gap on the right so cars could pass, yet Jesse stayed to their rear. Where the tips of their blades hit pavement, sparks flew into the sky. He drove to his hotel in a trail of fire.

TWO

OVER THE PHONE, JESSE BEGGED the lawyer's indulgence. He was sitting on his hotel bed fresh from the downstairs gym, sweat cooling on his skin. Could they find a way to zip through the legal business as quickly as possible so he could fly home before his business imploded? "My chef goes into meltdown if I ignore her for too long," Jesse said.

"Don't I know," Lieb said. "I go to the Cape five minutes, and my shop starts to stink like week-old tuna. Problem is, I'm on the fly, chum, depositions all day. Gotta set us up for tomorrow, 1 P.M., how'd that be?"

"Do I have a choice?"

"You could go fuck yourself." Lieb laughed at this. "Oh yeah," he said, "Tillton and Sons, I almost forgot. Near Ellsworth, wherever the hell that is. They're waiting for your call. My girl has the number."

"Tillton and Sons? What's that?"

Dead air, Lieb put him on hold. Jesse weighed the receiver in his hand. Owning the restaurant had taught him the intricacies of phone warfare—hanging up on hold announced your weakness, it lacked finesse. He brought the plastic to his cheek where it cooled his stubble.

The secretary came on and gave him a number, which Jesse wrote on the margin of the room-service menu. 603, that was

New Hampshire. Tillton and Sons, the idea seeped into him, was a funeral home. He carried the phone to the window and dialed the number, making an appointment for that afternoon.

The Charles lay two stories below, and by the banks a pair of runners paced the river. They pushed plumes of vapor in front of their masked faces as they ran through the brittle sunlight, their mouths open as if in surprise.

Fifteen years before, Jesse had run along the river course with Marty at the helm. Never in winter, though; winter was for fanatics. Their idea had been to run for pleasure, chasing the neural high. Jesse closed the shade.

The trip to New Hampshire passed through the industrial towns south of the White Mountains. The black car against the ice-white road, landscape of abandoned brick mill yards, churches that advertised bean suppers and bingo, boarded-up hot-dog shacks. Jesse kept one hand on his radio buttons and changed stations as they faded. FM here went in for power pop and metal. He boosted the volume until the dashboard hummed.

Three times he saw New Hampshire troopers giving out tickets. The taillights and bubble tops syncopated in violent blue, designed to quiver the heart. Good fortune can be willed, Marty once had told him. It's a matter of focus, you put your mind right and let go. Jesse had lacked a hopeful outlook, had refused the positive view. Now, as each tableau of car and cop swelled into sight, he leaned on the gas as hard as he was able. The Lincoln flew.

He passed Tillton and Sons twice before he realized he'd mistaken it for a residence. It was on the outskirts of

Ellsworth, where the town street changed to rural blacktop, a three-story Greek Revival with a small placard at the head of the long drive and a columned portico at the entrance. A sound of sobbing washed in muted waves from behind the front door while Jesse rang the bell and stamped his snowy feet on the mortuary doormat. "Welcome," the thing said, in large black letters.

He waited under the portico for an answer, shoving his scarf deeper into his collar, but the sorrow built and built with no hint of release. He rang again. Nothing. When he could think of no reason to return to his car, Jesse straightened his coat and let himself inside.

Within the large foyer a young woman was simultaneously bawling, smoking a cigarette, and attempting to pull a down jacket from a coat rack. Jesse couldn't turn away from her: her red face and bitten nails, grief carved into the hollows in her cheeks. How would it feel to hold her in his arms?

The woman apparently had put herself together in a hurry because her blouse was misbuttoned and her shirttails bunched at her waist. Amazing, the energy with which she rammed her arms into her jacket sleeves, shifting her cigarette from hand to hand. Jesse felt his face go red in embarrassment. His own loss had grown shamefully thin in comparison.

A man appeared in the hall, a middle-aged fellow in a proper black suit. His gait had a professional steadiness and he wore a small, pale rose in his lapel. He cooed—shh, shh—and his white hands stretched in comfort toward one and all. But the woman backed away from him and spat directly in his face as he drew near, derailing his motion. "Fuck you and fuck your shitty secretary job," she said. "Fuck this entire fucking place." The man's jaw worked silently as he wiped away the saliva dripping down the bridge of his nose.

The woman stormed the doorway where she halted and swept her arm across the entry table, scattering black-bordered leaflets to the floor. "See this, it's me leaving."

In final farewell, she stamped out her cigarette into the Persian runner and blew both of them a kiss goodbye.

Jesse realized he was clenching his fists as if her insults were directed at him. This was his first Christian funeral parlor—maybe hysteria was in long supply, even among employees. On closer observation, the director was much younger than he'd guessed, not too far out of his teens. Jesse was going to get everything wrong, it seemed. He took on the uncomfortable notion that he would be the one expected to lend solace.

"Not your most perfect day," he said. He gave the undertaker his name.

"Candace," the man sighed. "My assistant. I had to let her go, language, lateness, and so forth. No excuse for it. She has a troubled spirit, as you might guess." The man's attention looked past him to the spot where Candace had kissed the air goodbye.

He turned back to Jesse. "Yes. For Mr. Balakian. Good of you to come. Please, my apologies. James Tillton." The man extended a hand, noticed the glaze of spit on his fingers and let them drop. "My sincere condolences on your loss." Tillton's breath, Lord help him, smelled of peanut butter.

They went to the sales office, where the undertaker sat behind a writing table and filled out a printed form while Jesse inspected the several coffins fanned out between door and sitting area. He passed his hand over the glistening surface of one, warm from the overhead bulb. His fingertips left a smear.

Perhaps it was the overheated room, but when it was time to conclude his business, Jesse found himself unsteady on his feet, and he sat gratefully and poised Tillton's fat Mont Blanc over the document. It was hard to settle on any line in particular, though the word *DECEDENT* was repeated with nasty frequency. "What is this?" Jesse asked.

"Sorry, I thought you understood. Our agreement, Mr. Kerf. Goods and services. I've learned over the years to dispense with the business side first. Puts a perspective on it. I find that important."

"Perspective," Jesse said. "That's what I like. The whole panorama."

Tillton brought out some full-color brochures and asked Jesse what kind of ceremony he wanted.

"Ceremony? None. No ceremony. Marty won't care about a ceremony."

"Without explicit instructions, we can never speak for the deceased, Mr. Kerf. What we provide, then, is for the living."

"No ceremony."

"The casket?" Tillton's gaze alighted on a dark brown number to Jesse's left. Jesse appraised the eager tilt of the man's chin. He shook his head. No casket.

Tillton's eyelids flickered briefly. Cremation was a perfectly acceptable alternative. They had a selection of urns for every wallet.

"Mr. Tillton. Give me what's simplest. What's easiest. No muss, no fuss."

"The least expensive, I imagine?"

Jesse found a place to sign and scrawled his name. "Exactly. I knew my friend. Unless you do Viking funerals on Lake Winnipesaukee, I'm sure he'd want me to spend my money on some single malt and raise a glass and nothing more.

Tillton slid the form back, made a few notations, the jaw in motion. "A simple cremation. Plain container, $1,300. You may pick up the cremains in the morning.

Jesse rose, stumbling slightly. His foot had fallen asleep and he knocked it sharply against the table leg. A little pain was good for the system, the flare along the nerves.

"Payment in advance, if you don't mind," Tillton said.

"Will you take a California check?"

The undertaker sniffed and informed him that checks were not permitted. Credit cards, however, were perfectly all right, and while Jesse signed the slip, the undertaker brought up the subject of a showing.

"A showing?"

"Thought you might want to say goodbye to your friend. It's not required, of course. All right if you decline. Some don't have the stomach for it."

"No. A showing. That sounds good."

The coffin next to Jesse shone with lemon oil. He remembered the smell from his childhood and his mother's constant campaign to keep their house agleam. The image of Jesse's face bent around the curving wood. "Let's go," he said. "Let's have our showing." He tried a step toward the door and found his foot no longer tingled.

Marty's face was the faded umber of old piano ivory. It rested on a field of mauve silk, and the mouth revealed a thoughtful pose, lips slightly apart, a hint of teeth. Keeping a secret, perhaps, or hiding a lie. The late afternoon sun gilded the features with a rosy bloom. Life in death, so the Bible promised.

Jesse edged his chair a few inches nearer to the coffin. Marty's hair was absurdly lustrous, blacker than he remembered, falling in curls that seemed to billow against the silk. Jesse leaned in. The interior was doused with perfume that overlaid but could not mask Marty's own rich aroma, the harsh animal scent of death. The smell was dense and provocative and offered a reminder: end of the day, we turn to trash.

Jesse waited for the overall picture to disengage into its individual parts, a trick from his time as an art major, a concentration of the eye. In such a state he'd stare at the model for an hour and tease the body out of the lines his pencil made, considering volume and space alone. His favorite had been Greta, a blonde.

A glint moved across the coffin's brass fittings. Dark soon, the same wintry emptiness he'd driven through last night. The viewing room window gave out onto a vast meadow that was fading from sight with the passage of the sun. It got darker here than in California, was this possible?

Shadows traversed the mahogany sides of the box. The wood was splintered at the bottom edge and mended more than once—a viewing coffin, rented by the hour, used how many times before, ten, twenty, a hundred? The half lid revealed the body down to the top button of its suit where the crossed hands lay against the chest. The shirt cuffs bore tan stains at the rim, used in a previous wearing, he guessed, a package deal with the rental casket. The cowboy boots, Jesse wondered. What had become of Marty's boots?

He grabbed at the closed section of the lid and it flew open with a snap and fell away from his grip. Marty's legs rattled against the sides of the box.

The body was naked from the waist down. The clothing ended a few inches above the belt-line, a bleached dickey beneath a false front of a coat that buckled around the body with elastic straps. Yes—exactly right, a practical solution yet sly, the sort Marty would devise. It did him honor.

A patch of soiled cloth covered the groin, and tea-colored bruises mottled the bottoms of the legs where the blood had settled. A yellow and blue wound in the left side bulged with gauze. The spleen—such a small injury, but enough to bleed out Marty's life. The body was otherwise unmarked, but its feet were bare.

"I come from a long line of carpet thieves and stealers of sheep," Marty had liked to say, waving his grand Armenian nose in your face as proof. From this angle, Jesse could see the cotton that filled the nostrils. Sometimes the line ends. Jesse closed both coffin doors. Marty Balakian had been his friend and his enemy. Now he was nothing—an artifact, a thing. Jesse would ask about the boots before he left.

THREE

JESSE. HEY, JESSE. Look at him moseying around my kitchen hunting for my coffee. Jet lag and a heavy conscience runs a backhoe through your REM—the man can't do what's needed without some good caffeine. It's in the back cupboard, Little Brother, in an airtight canister, stainless steel, just like I taught you. Bingo, got it first try, you're doing fine. The grinder's in the cabinet to the left. See how the boy still takes my lead? Same as always.

I like the coat—he popped for cashmere, very smooth. And that gray at the temples, those serious lines by the corners of his mouth—Jesse's aged well. Buffed up in L.A., no question. It's a requirement out there, is how I hear it, a necessary element. He makes a good impression. I forgot he was that tall.

He looks tense, though, his neck and shoulders all in knots. It's a mesh of trigger points, the upper back, he's got to be in pain. Too bad—I guess I fucked him up. Hey, Jesse, take care of how you eat and sleep. Stamina is key and you're bound to burn through every ounce before you're done, trust me. It goes with the job description—Next of Kin. You don't have to thank me. De nada.

I used to make him laugh. He needed to—he had a deficiency, a vitamin lack. A bad chromosome. He took a push or he'd forget he was alive. One time, we laughed for an hour, hardly stopped for a breath.

We were stoned—weren't we always? Stoned quite often in the old days—grass, hash, a merry catalog of alkaloids. Then the old days ended, but a few of us didn't abandon our habits, a few of us bravely ventured on. We saw our duty. Till the '80s. The '80s brought the best of us to our knees. Reagan, Wall Street, don't make me give you the list.

OK, for accuracy's sake, I switched over to bourbon, top-shelf exclusively, Blanton's or Knob Creek. Whiskey's a nice body high—that smoky flavor, a taste of carcinogens at the back of the throat, the tough-guy kick. Bourbon meshed with the '80s, didn't it? Weed, I don't know, I couldn't hack it suddenly. Too much something—excess wattage, maybe, too much particularity when I wanted mush. Look, we're born with how many brain cells? A billion or two, who cares, more than we need. I was pleased to offer the donation and bourbon was happy to receive.

We hadn't made the move to California, Jesse and me, the night we laughed. California was in our future but we didn't know it. We were friends, we hung out—Chinatown lunches, rock shows on the Common, street demos—we attended to the present. Somerville friends, we had that link, local boys.

Jesse was in college at Northeastern. He had a scholarship and took art classes, mooned over the models, as I recall, worried his sweet mom and dad. It was an ugly scene, Northeastern—trolley cars slamming on the rails, and the Huntington Y down the block, its torn-up pool tables, riffraff on the steps eyeing marks as they walked by. Jesse's dorm room was a killer—concrete 180 degrees out all the windows and a fair view of the projects. Moderating the asphalt required a high percentage of Jesse being elsewhere, so he slept through lecture halls and ignored Friday night mixers, slid papers under his teachers' doors weeks after they were due. I did my bit as general helpmate and nasty influence. More than a decade I had on the boy—I offered the perspective of years.

The night we laughed, we were at my place in North Cambridge, wasted on black Afghan hash. Two tokes sit on you like two tons. The subject falls onto that guy, that Japanese guy, he was a writer, wasn't he, an actor, too, a movie director? The man was major in Japan. He died—a suicide, but designed with an eye to style, with élan. There were many lovely features to that particular demise—disembowelment, beheading, political theory.

Somehow the guy has a private army, so he tries a coup to bring back the Golden Age. Who wouldn't? But naturally, the coup goes sour: hello *seppuku,* hello entrails and decapitation. It was all part of the plan.

Nevertheless, rumor has it the man failed to make a good death, a personal weakness at the finale. The Japanese have criteria, don't they, high expectations, and our guy fumbled. Jesse can't see beyond the failure. For him the writer's poor result defines the event from top to bottom.

I say the specifics aren't important, they're annoying. What we require is right brain only—coup, sword, death, the overall scheme. Jesse refuses, he has to flay the topic inside out, to see what we can learn. OK, I'll play along, I say, let's be Talmudic. There is one question that has me confused. The head, I ask. How many bounces when it hits the floor?

Jesse laughs—it takes him by surprise. He opens his mouth and roars. Laughter swallows him up—it's kind of beautiful to watch, the autonomous nervous system in control. Guess what: I am laughing too. I can't stop, and neither can he. We laugh until we don't know where we are or who we are or why. One hour. That's how it was—I joked and Jesse laughed. I laughed back.

A good death, Jesse. Don't be too fussy, now.

He was due at Lieb's office in an hour. Jesse foresaw a stack of documents to sign and another check to write. Loss was a business that operated with its own rules and conditions like everything else. The lawyer's growl resounded in Jesse's ear, his gutter mouth, the snort. The morning was destined to try his patience; it would be a form of torture. But afterward there'd be the packing up and selling off and then home free. At the restaurant this moment, Manuel and the boys would be proofing the ciabatta on its second rise.

The box of ashes stood on Marty's kitchen table, fresh from the trunk where it had ridden next to the lizard boots. Cremains—a word for the ages, one the mortician had insisted on repeating as often as possible. Jesse shook the box back and forth and heard a sifting, an indistinct rattle. Marty's smile had gold in it, he remembered. Jesse carried the box from room to room, wondering where it belonged.

In the past, Marty's talk had been full of houses—caves on Crete, palapas on the Sea of Cortez—the houses they'd live in, the women who'd warm their beds and cook them spicy tidbits, experiences like a string of shining pearls. "Tell me where to get in line," Jesse had said. "What do I have to do? I'm packed."

Marty sighed. "We do nothing, we take our time. Fate drives the bus, not us."

Jesse studied himself in Marty's bathroom mirror, his face so white and trembling it seemed his tan had faded in a single day. The world is built on actions, not on fate. Did Marty ever learn?

He brought the box of ashes to the bedroom floor where it caught a stripe of morning light. A stale scent drifted up from Marty's scattered T-shirts and jeans and the mildewed sateen of his quilt, from the window curtains mapped with cobwebs. Coins were tossed in all directions, glints of silver on the dark wood floor. Jesse evened the bed sheets and squared the coverlet into a bundle ready for Goodwill.

He thought it prudent to put together an accounting for the lawyer: kitchen table, three chairs, futon, desk, laptop computer, and of course the books, a list filling less than a page in his Day Runner. The computer was propped on Marty's desk, its screen open and locked on password control. The glass surface reflected ghostly particles of Jesse's movements as though it were keeping him under surveillance.

For now, all that was left was to air out the room, and the draft brought in the homely smells of wood smoke and washday chlorine. Marty's view looked out onto a familiar Somerville prospect of backyard clotheslines and snow-caked religious statuary. Above Jesse icicles lined the eave like soldiers. The largest one was broader than his arm at its root and twice as long; its blue-white skin captured the swift motion of clouds.

Jesse hoisted himself onto the sill. Now he discerned the icicle's flaws: veins of sooty black staining every layer. He rapped the ice with a knuckle and it shivered, then Jesse struck again with all his strength. The icicle hurled past as though he'd let fly an arrow. Its broken remnants scattered across six feet of hard-packed snow.

Jesse drove toward Lieb's faster than the roads allowed, and he rechecked Marty's watch to verify the time. The Rolex had been lying in a bowl of ticket stubs and loose change, an Oyster Chronometer worth thousands, just the thing for the driver of a Lincoln. He grunted with pleasure as he admired the lump of calibrated chrome. It was a fake, it had to be. Why hadn't he thought of it before, the fuzzy quality to the logo and a clamminess in how the bracelet pressed onto his skin. If he weren't careful, it would turn him green. At a stop sign, Jesse brought his wrist up to his face and felt against the sensitive flesh of his ear the barest hum.

FOUR

THE WOMAN IN THE PAINTING had been drawn as a hollow-ribbed nude with prominent nipples and a dangerous patch of black at the join of her thighs. Her scowl offered the impression it was the process of law that had stripped her bare, and Jesse wondered whether Lieb had chosen her as inspiration or threat. Beneath her stare, he listened to the cadence of the argument coming from the lawyer's executive suite.

The shouting had gone on for twenty minutes, shouting so loud and abusive, the receptionist was forced to offer apologies. Jesse told her not to worry—lawyers were like generals. They took pleasure by reducing you in advance to a state of fearful and needy fatigue.

The office windows opened onto the Public Garden. The panes were stamped with flakes—the earlier sprinkling had ripened into a sizable presence, and Jesse traced the crawl of vehicles through the blizzard, the blur of taillights, the caterwaul of horns that rose two stories. At the corner, a traffic cop was curled into the wind as though in prayer.

Jesse's neck was killing him—every mile he'd flown and driven charted along the spine—and when the receptionist went off to Xerox, he knelt to the floor for a round of push-ups. He looked up and smiled as she returned to tell him Lieb was ready, but there were fifteen to go and he wanted to finish.

The sleek colors of the woman's outfit gave her a youthful flourish, yet Jesse felt her soft regard as motherly.

Lieb waited for him in his office doorway. He wore a suit of fine-spun gray flannel and new Nike trainers, and he bounced on his feet like a bantam fighter coming out of his corner. He spread his arms and hauled Jesse into an embrace and muttered fierce syllables of condolence. Jesse found his arms dangling against the lawyer's back.

"Tall motherfucker, aren't you?" Lieb said by way of introduction. His teeth were small and faultlessly white.

They took seats at opposing sides of a reproduction Chippendale desk, and Lieb held up a palm for silence in order to snatch up his buzzing telephone receiver and launch a barrage of invective and legal arcana. You had to hand it to the man, he knew how to lay on the pressure. His way of moving displayed a touch of ballet—how he thrust his fist in the air as he talked, the arc of his sleeve in its thousand-dollar wool.

Jesse reached out and depressed the telephone's hang-up switch. "I'm easily distracted," he said. "Let's get on to our business before I lose track of why I came."

The lawyer's eyes bulged momentarily. He lit a cigar and sat back to give Jesse the benefit of his sober regard. "Take a little advice from me," he said. "Business I'm in, I have experience with this death and dying circumstance. Some people, it brings out the worst. Others, the opposite. How does it go? The better angels of our nature. Whichever way you slice and dice, it's a crap shoot, so you want to ease up, Big Guy. You want to be open to the upside on this. Take it from me, there's always an upside."

"That's what Marty liked to say, but I was hard to convince. I haven't changed."

Lieb rubbed a crust of ash into a crystal ashtray he had moved into place. "You believe in God, Jesse? Cause I do. Don't ask me why, the scum I see day in, day out. Something in you gets hungry for it, a belief like that. At night I can almost hear it, like there's a heart beating somewhere. The beating doesn't stop, that's what's so amazing. In a hard world, you can take comfort." The lawyer paused. The buttons on his phone were alight and he gazed longingly in their direction.

Jesse brought out his checkbook. "Thanks for the guidance," he said. "The universal heartbeat. I'll make sure to note it down so I won't forget. But now, tell me what's needed here and I'll write the number. That shouldn't be so difficult."

"Fuck. A man in a hurry."

The lawyer set down his cigar and pulled a file from the stack before him, peeling a shred of tobacco from his tongue. "I can't be completely accurate yet, but give or take a half a percent, eight point three."

"I don't follow."

"$8.3 million. It depends on the bond rate at the time you redeem, but like I said, give or take, you'll cash out at $8.3 mil after taxes, more if you float the stocks a while and the market holds." Lieb smiled his pointy smile. "It's all yours, every dime. That's why I asked if you believe in God. Cause he fucking believes in you."

A bead of sweat dripped along Jesse's rib cage. "You're joking. Have you seen how Marty lived?"

"Never had the pleasure. We maintained a relationship of purely business—lunch once a quarter when he walked me through the tally. Sometimes we played squash before. He had a backhand like a fucking cruise missile."

"Tally?"

Lieb revolved the folder so Jesse might see. Bound inside were computer spreadsheets representing several years of accounting. "InfoCon—Marty's business." Lieb explained. "You don't know diddly, do you?"

Jesse skipped his hand down the columns. Numbers overran the pages.

"Your pal, Big Guy, was a fucking genius. He was creator and sole owner of the largest term paper mill in the known universe. Ran the whole thing through computers. Modems, uplinks, don't ask me what the fuck it means, downloads. He served an international clientele. No faces, that was key. Deniability all around, not that it was needed. Thing was a hundred percent legal."

"Term papers?" The size of Jesse's ignorance felt immense.

"You got any idea how many students want the degree but don't want to crack a book? How much they'll pay for the privilege of subcontracting out? Marty sold them term papers and called it research. Twelve bucks a page. Eighteen custom work—twenty-four with footnotes and indexing. Something like a hundred writers on call, half with Ph.D.s, Harvard, Yale, all the Ivies. Your pal was particular."

Lieb drew on his cigar and produced a smoke ring that hovered between them. "Want one? Not every day you hit the jackpot." He nudged aside a file and came up with a fresh corona, which Jesse held clumsily. There was a ritual, he remembered it dimly from the movies, you turned the thing by your ear before lighting up. Listening for what?

"Don't wait all day, pal. That's a Davidoff, the finest Cuban they got. A guy I know makes the trip to Toronto twice a month."

Jesse slipped the pointier end in his mouth and allowed the man to light him. Smooth and harsh at the same time, the cigar watered his vision and he tasted salt with the smoke. To clear his thinking, he closed his eyes. He saw rows and rows of dusty books. Each loss came with its own shape and smell.

In benediction, Lieb described his last encounter with Marty on the Harvard Club squash court, complete with forehand displays. Jesse listened and nodded and smoked. Computer ink and ash soiled his fingertips, and he wiped them clean on his pants the best he could.

Money. Some people say it's a drug, but they never say what drug, do they? A tang at the back of the mouth, lips and temples pumping with metallic glee. Let me set the record straight: commerce is like meth. Good crystal—not that crank they give you nowadays. Stuff that opens the doors of paradise.

Here's the joke—I lost my facility for spending. Limp-dicked for consumption, I admit to a weakness there. The desire for things just dropped away—hence my dusty floors and faded walls and grimy clothes, hence the Somerville locale. Judge me by what I accomplished, Jesse, not by my debris.

Can I tell you how much it got me off—the making of money, watching it grow like a garden, watching it spread like a disease? I felt it in my body like a crawling in the blood. A simple game with a simple way of keeping score—more is better and most is better still.

Genius, Lieb called my setup, and maybe it was, once I identified what I was selling, once I clarified my attack, once I figured out my market. You look a trifle green, Little Brother, is it the cigar? You don't inhale, it's dangerous, nobody give you the word?

My business, do you see it yet—electrons jingling on the public wire, all that information zipping back and forth? Ones and zeros passing by my pocket and dumping dollars. Computer code—it had simplicity and cleanliness, a quality of being basic, strings of numbers like a rock or a tree. I'd be kidding if I didn't cop to being proud.

You seem freaked out, though, and who could blame you, hardly watching the road, the Lincoln weaving through the storm. All that money's locked your mind up tight. Come on, it's a nor'easter you're cruising through. Both eyes on the road, hands at ten and two—one car crash per family is plenty to satisfy the gods.

You're going to have to take some time to soak it in, get accustomed to a new order of being. I just hopscotched you a couple dozen pay grades, Little Brother—moved you as far away from where we got our start as you can be. It's a pretty universe you've landed in, though by my counting you were on that road before you got the call to come back East: car phones and beach houses, art on the walls somebody else tells you to buy, designer clothes, designer digs, designer friends. Invest my dough with smarts, and you'll never have to work another day unless you want to. Or you could clone your restaurant and multiply my holdings ten times over, sail off farther than I ever could. I can picture a whole chain of places with your name, crowds of well-dressed and happy citizens nibbling at your wood-grilled tuna, your puttanesca, your roasted duck with garlic confit. We made confit together, remember when? You and me and Isabel, our first year in Santa Cruz. Two pounds of garlic, I showed you how to clean the skins. They were airborne, feather-light, like papery ash on our hair and flesh and beards, ash on the nape of Isabel's neck. I kissed her spotless.

Rain played on the kitchen window, remember? The earliest rain of October, I can hear it, hard as fists. We put Dylan on multiple repeat, *Blonde on Blonde*, and danced, and you tripped over your shoelaces drunk on cabernet and fellow feeling. We danced and the garlic hummed in the pan, caramel in the air, a smell thick enough to swallow. We danced in the gray light and shat garlic for a week. Do you remember?

Ah, Jesse, your left eyelid has a tremor that wasn't there this morning. Grief's a burden but it can be borne. Time will do its job, I have no doubt. But money, money stirs up trouble, doesn't it, money muddies the soup. Eight-point-three million—the figure has heft, wouldn't you agree, round and large and confusing? I wonder if you do—if you'll keep together or fall apart. Trust old Marty. I won't desert you in your hour.

Success. That's what I sold, Jesse. Success without effort. Success by the pound. InfoCon was how I wanted it, legally clean and morally complex. The world's a market and everything finds its price. Love even. Ask Jesus.

The police had ordered drivers off the road. Ice glazed over the lane divisions on the roadway, and the Lincoln bucked against Jesse's control in lurching shudders. He carried himself through the storm with the taste of tobacco filming his breath.

He did not want to stop—not at the hotel room with its over-bright lighting and faux marble and pecan furniture, not at the dim, book-filled apartment on Dooley Street. Keeping in motion was the idea—driving until he ran out of gas or out of storm, driving until his thinking conformed to the world of white outside his windshield.

For a while he crisscrossed Back Bay without a thought of where he was, but then he pictured the offices of InfoCon—he could drive there. Lieb had given him a set of keys and an address in a factory district near MIT. At InfoCon there would be a chair, a telephone, a terrain of objects with recognizable dimensions and sizes and forms. Maybe someone would be working still and tell him about Marty and his recent days. Jesse found the turn for Mass. Ave., and he passed the Institute cutting grooves through mounding snow. He was the only moving thing on a four-lane street.

The neighborhood appeared in the first blush of economic revival: its brick factory buildings housed cafes and offices in designs that buttressed the durable utility of the past to a promise of tasteful acquisition. At the center of the block, InfoCon's flapping awning threatened to tear itself to shreds. Jesse wrestled with the crank until his fingers went numb, but he managed only to bring the thing halfway down.

Marty's vestibule was buttery with furnace heat, and as Jesse mounted the stairs, running now, his ear quickened to the sound of a string quartet descending from the office level. Beethoven—Marty loved the moody later stuff when syphilis, he claimed, had cast its imprint on the music. Opening the door shot days of mail across the planking floor. Jesse slipped on envelopes and circulars; some of them stuck to his wet shoes.

The room was a disappointment, a cheat, a looming cavern lacking furniture and staff, lacking everything except the expensive radio that rested on a dusty window ledge. The place smelled of damp wood and the exhalations of the heating system, and along the floor, the shadows of rusting bolts and stanchions kept company with the blackened outlines of the machines that once had dominated the room. InfoCon's office was nothing more than a mail drop, a false front to deflect interest in the man himself. The music was hooked onto a timer—Marty's consummate touch.

Jesse collected as many envelopes as would fit into his pockets—two or three trips and he'd have them all. He decided to leave the radio playing. Opus 131—the adagio was one of his favorite melodies. He drove back to his hotel humming the tune and wondering if the snow would fall all night.

FIVE

Jesse ordered a room service dinner and wasted the afternoon in bed watching TV, flipping from channel to channel. Shows swooped on and off the screen with an energetic pop as though violence were necessary to the transition. On ABC, a somber Oprah Winfrey had her arms around a weeping girl.

By 6:30, it was time to phone his restaurant, and while he waited for the connection, Jesse muted the TV and switched to a channel playing wrestling. The tumble of flesh played in dumb-show as the telephone chimed in California.

He imagined Helena leaning against the wall by the eight-burner Viking, her blond ponytail drooping after the midday crush, her chef's linen stained generously, her temper frayed. By now, she would have flung her apron into the hamper, unsnapped the top button of her pants, and bundled her white T-shirt above her waist. She would smell of olives and almond soap and onions. On the TV, a wrestler in red was screaming at the ref.

Helena was eating lunch and she adorned her talk with mumbles and sighs. She missed him, everybody missed him, Copain was a disaster without him, who said he could take time off? The new waitress quit mid-shift, the red-haired one, Terry something, and the wine distributor blew it for the gazillionth time, they were still laying on the chardonnay when everybody knows chardonnay's over. But the osso buco flew out the door two days running. The new sauce of orange gremolata and simmered marrow killed.

"Not literally, I hope," Jesse said.

Helena snorted. "Are you having fun? You're not allowed."

"I think I'm OK. I'm tired. It's snowing."

"Snowing? Where are you? You said personal business, I thought you were staying home with the '89 P&L and eating Doritos."

"I went to Boston."

"Please don't say you're checking out what's-her-name at the Four Seasons, Amelia Benton. I don't want another body on the line. I'm all the maniac you can possibly afford."

Jesse heard the squeak of Helena's clogs against the kitchen floor. After service, she paced like a well-run animal, an Irish setter perhaps, sloe-eyed and shaggy and high-strung. He shifted the receiver to his other ear.

"The trip has nothing to do with Copain. Old history. Times gone by."

Onscreen, a man in tights sat on another's head. The loser held a transparent gaze of comfortable resolve; Jesse thought of the cattle ranches up on Highway 5, docile beasts oblivious to their eventual destruction.

"A guy told me today he thought God was a heartbeat," Jesse said. "What do you think?"

"I think you need to hurry home to those who love you. Bad weather is messing with your mind. Tomorrow's the Hillerman anniversary, a hundred and twenty-seven of their most fabulous friends. You remember Alexis Hillerman? We're doing clean food—that's what she wants. No sauces, no spices, no skin, oil, fat, dairy, or nuts. What's left, tell me, please. The woman weighs ninety-five pounds and goes to Puerto Vallarta every year to recycle her blood. They take it out and wash away the toxins, then pump it back in. Erases a decade off the dermis, she says. If you want, I can ask her."

"Ask her what?"

"If God is a heartbeat. The woman's son took Michael Milken's daughter to the junior prom. She's probably tight with God, too, bubby."

Jesse fixed on the TV screen: the man on the ground performed a flip and now sat on the first guy's head. Jesse hit the off button and the image receded. "Helena, about my trip," he said, wondering where to begin, how far back.

Helena cut him off at once. "No. Stop and think for a second, sweetie. I don't have mental space for whatever you want to dump. I'll lose my edge, which I cannot afford, and neither can you. I'm exhausted and I stink up to my elbows of lobster nage. I need a shower and a twenty-minute nap and then there's dinner. Rack of lamb's on special, and the wood oven has a case of hot spots. I don't have room for anything but the work at hand."

Once Jesse had seen Helena plate nine separate dinners in less than a minute, then swing to the Viking to flip a pair of omelets in absolute synchrony—all the while berating a tardy dishwasher in gutter Spanish. Sometimes, at the end of a difficult night, she shut herself inside the walk-in and vented deep howls. She emerged and wiped her tears and tipped her baseball hat to the kitchen crew, smiling a challenge no one cared to pick up.

He told her their talk could wait until he returned. The blizzard was beating against the windows so that the entire room appeared to throb. "I'm wondering, though," Jesse said. "Where exactly in Puerto Vallarta? I want the address. I want names. I want instructions."

Helena's telephone laughter twisted into the receiver, a soft and tiny thing. She sent kisses goodbye. Tomorrow morning, Jesse decided, he would go to Marty's apartment and shovel the walk for Mrs. Folari. It had been years since he'd had a shovel in his hands. He could play the good boy, too.

Clearing the walk absorbed half an hour of steady effort. Jesse devoted himself to the felicities of bend and lift, the stripe of dark pavement brought to light, the bitter cold numbing his fingertips and ears, bracing his lungs. He was wearing Marty's boots. They were an especially fine pair of black Luccheses whose lizard scales rippled as he walked. Jesse couldn't recall the man in anything else—no, not even for basketball, though how could that be true? Boots gave rigor to the step. They pointed the toes like the muzzle of a gun.

While Jesse shoveled, Mrs. Folari kept vigil from the window—her black dress moved now and then at the edge of the living room shade. She maintained her distance, however, a matter of propriety Jesse decided not to try to understand.

It was nearly noon when he set himself to dismantling Marty's apartment, making and filling and stacking book boxes in a constant flow of movement. Doing the work himself offered a form of exchange for his multimillion-dollar reward, a contribution in kind. In his experience, numbers so large had a habit of turning vague and conceptual. Physical labor lay a shine on the figure Jesse could not ignore.

He slept at the apartment to conserve energy and time, breaking at midday to scavenge castoff cartons from neighborhood package stores. He liked the solidity of wine boxes—the ones for champagne were the strongest. Marty's brand was Veuve Clicquot, and Jesse rooted them out, creamy orange containers with a Rococo script and a slick air of celebration. He became well known to the liquor sellers of the community, a subject of jokes.

Labeled as to contents, the boxes marched along Marty's living room walls and then in aisles Jesse created by dismantling the shelves. They balanced against each other in stacks that shifted with his footfall, often toppling with a crash that jolted the loose floorboards. Sometimes they fell for no reason, when Jesse was in the kitchen or the bathroom or asleep. Four nights running, Jesse went to bed with the stench of mold and magic marker ink upon his skin. He lay in bed and waited for the sound.

In the kitchen, nothing escaped the trash: spices, cookware, pantry items, none of it worth saving except an unopened fifth of Blanton's. Blanton's, most certainly the best and most expensive bourbon on the market. Jesse rolled a hit on his tongue and a sharp fog collected momentarily behind his eyes.

Time past, it was scotch, not bourbon, single malt, of rare unpronounceable variety. Marty had demonstrated how it should be taken—neat, in water glasses, standing up. As men. Jesse had not foreseen the bitter taste, and had finished grimly, feeling failure. Now he put the bourbon aside for the trip home. With the fake Rolex and the boots, it was the only thing he wanted.

By the end of the week, everything had been done but phoning the charities and garbage men to come for their respective shares. Jesse carted his final bundle backward toward the entry, a large lawn and leaf bag full of Marty's bedroom belongings. He had stuffed the bag too full, thrown the desk lamp in with clothes, and as he shuffled along, half carrying and half dragging, each bump and snag filled the air with dust. Near the door, Jesse's strength faltered and he let the bag collapse with a rustle and the frail sound of splintering glass. He left it where it fell for the Salvation Army to cart away.

On the last evening, Mrs. Folari knocked on the upstairs door and led Jesse down to a farewell dinner. Roast capon with fresh rosemary and pancetta—he had not known how to refuse, nor wanted to, he had to admit. He'd spent more time alone than he was used to and missed the talk and lively energy of his restaurant. Missed the family feeling.

The landlady listened to music while she cooked, and it took a few moments for Jesse to understand she had chosen the same doleful Beethoven he had heard at Marty's office. The coincidence worked on him—soon there would be signs and portents, things flying through the air.

He kept Mrs. Folari company at her kitchen counter and to busy his hands, Jesse took over chopping cherry peppers for the gravy. Helena was capable of producing tiny dice in a bright blur of knife, but he was making a mess of it and pepper essence splattered the nap of his dusty sweater. The small nicks on his chapped hands felt the bite of the juice.

The old woman smiled as the cello played its lovely line, and then she fussed a brown lump of innards from the capon's carcass. She muttered an imprecation in Italian as she cleaned herself against her apron. Beneath its muslin bodice Jesse saw the outline of a cross.

"We used to kill them fresh when I was a girl," Mrs. Folari announced. "Wring their skinny necks. It's the supermarket now, everything wrapped in plastic like the chicken's maybe going to fly away." She inspected Jesse's efforts with suspicion and picked up his knife without a word, slashing the remaining peppers into large hunks that she carried in her hands to the stove.

Jesse took some respite in the living room where the stereo winked its lights from within an old oak cabinet. It was all brushed chrome surfaces and digital read-out and must have set the woman back thousands. The notion struck him that Marty had given Mrs. Folari the stereo—and the quartet it was playing. He saw below the amplifier four shelves of compact discs.

"I told him not to waste his money on an old woman."

Mrs. Folari's eyeglasses were wet with pasta steam, her fingers hunting for the crucifix that touched her bosom. Thinking to reach out to her, Jesse stepped toward the stove; she looked in need. But he stalled, sensing in his face a vital rush of color. Liar—my need, mine.

The landlady's false teeth made a circuit in her mouth. She gave her pan of escarole an assertive shake; cast iron rang against the burner. "Foolishness. I told him he was off his rocker. 'Let me be crazy,' he says. 'I'm good at it.' Who talks like that? But he won't let me say no. You know how Marty is."

Jesse nodded his head slowly. "Yes," he said, "I do," but he was unsure whether it was true. Sighing, the woman opened the oven to baste the roasting bird, releasing into the room a sweet, greasy scent.

The music had played out and Jesse went back to choose a new disc. The bright plastic cases clicked along his finger as he squinted at the titles. Christ, most of them were still inside their wrappers. He would play the Beethoven once more. Why not? You could listen to it a hundred times and fail to penetrate its depths.

It started up, and Jesse waited for dinner at the empty table resting his arms upon the cool linen cloth. Behind him, he heard Mrs. Folari's crooning and the drumming of her wooden spoon inside her skillet. A tender sensation brushed against his legs; the linen fringe listing with the draft. Jesse was crying as steadily as he breathed and his face was lit with surprise. The old woman did not hear and kept on with her singing.

SIX

1973

MARTY WEAVES HIS CAR THROUGH TRAFFIC as though every second saved is the most important second of his life. He cheerleads himself through gear changes, ramming his shifter through the notches—even his lips are in motion, the column of air within his lungs. Settle down, Jesse wants to tell him, can't you see the party going on two feet beyond your nose? Useless—the man's a hundred percent destination and zero ride.

Mild spring temperatures have gathered the residents of Cambridge in all their factions. Jaywalkers and Frisbee players and skateboard lunatics mob a side street in Harvard Square, and strains of Hare Krishna and sidewalk mandolin rise over the sound of the Volvo's troubled muffler. Jesse rolls down his window to catch a weak vee of sunlight on his elbow. It should be warmer, Marty says. Skylab, he believes, is fucking with the weather.

A couple sitting on the curb are kissing with great seriousness, and as Jesse turns to face them, they separate and look on one another as though meeting for the first time, then switch into a fresh position, tongues a spot of sunlit pink. That would make a painting, the pink against a granite field. He could knife the colors from the palette, smash pigment on the canvas. If he were painting. Jesse holds upon the lovers until the car turns the corner toward the Charles.

On the far side of the river, his class has already begun. Being late is a feeling to appreciate—a tug of liberation and foreboding that adds definition to an ordinary day. Jesse tips his head out the window and the soft afternoon breeze feathers his hair against his shoulders. He'll be lucky if he sees school at all.

Along the riverbank, three women drowse under the willows, and Jesse examines their easy sleep as though it's a dance step he might learn. Lately his nights are uncertain and poisoned by unremembered dreams. The burden of an empathetic soul, is Marty's theory. So long as American warplanes drop bombs on Asian hamlets, slumber will be disturbed coast to coast.

"Hey, I think that's Caroline." Marty stands on his brakes. With a glance into the rearview mirror, he tucks his T-shirt into his pants, smooths the image on his chest, a cop performing artificial respiration on a child. "Some Would Call Him Pig," in typeface underneath.

"I'm doomed," Jesse says. "Painting class is waiting."

"Life is waiting," says Marty, already out the door.

Jesse leans against the hood to soak engine heat into the sore under-muscle of his thigh. They spent the morning shooting baskets, and Marty loves to leave his mark—today the tender impression of a knee. Across the street the sunbathers seem eagerly awake; their pale skin flickers as the wind rustles through the branches. The sound of laughter blends with shuttling leaves.

"I know this dude who'll loan you seven paintings for sixty bucks," Marty tells Jesse a few minutes later as they shoot across the Mass. Ave. Bridge. "His thing is color field, and he likes to go big, spray-paints these giant shapes in monotone acrylic, big black square, big green triangle, big red diamond, nothing but geometry and scale. Maybe that'll prime your pump, get you back in the studio for real. My guy guarantees a B or money back."

"Color field grinds my teeth. If I'm going to lose my cherry, let's dig up some figurative pieces, Pop or super-realism. Something with flesh tones and sex appeal on the canvas."

"You think this is a buyer's market?"

"I know what grinds my teeth."

Marty strokes his beard. "Color field or nothing, sweetie, flip the coin. Just don't confuse inertia with higher moral purpose."

"Wouldn't think of it," Jesse says. He thumbs the radio buttons, impatient for bounce and melody; he twirls the volume knob as high as it will go. Pink, definitely, he decides. In oil. Layers of pink over a gray ground, but the pink, aglow, aloft. Just floating there, two tongues.

Not far from the university studios, Marty pulls up at the Back Bay House of Pizza. The afternoon visit is part of their daily schedule, Jesse waiting shotgun in the car while his friend attends to his career. The shop's domestic qualities are in absentia: a riot grate over the windows, a pocked logo of a half-crazed pizza man above the door, yet by the storefront window Marty buttons on a lambskin vest to clean up his appearance. With his braids flapping against the leather, the man looks about as businesslike as Tonto.

The entrance produces an immediate yield of noise and movement. Marty and his Uncle Dikran have been feuding for months and it doesn't take more than hello to bump them into war. Through the window glass, they converge into a unity of waving arms and rising voices.

Six nights a week their bicycle crews hawk Italian sandwiches the length of B.U.'s dormitory row. Dikran churns out the fresh torpedo bread and the meatballs and sausage, and Marty sees to the schedules and the books and weighs a whip hand, when required, on the labor. They pull four grand a month out of the business and Marty itches to expand. He knows a guy who knows a guy who'll front a franchise corporation out of Delaware. Success is fated—guaranteed, Marty insists. He sees them nationwide within a year.

"There are eighteen kinds of insanity," Uncle D has gone on record. "And nationwide, you better believe, goddamn, is one. I reject your guaranteed."

From the back seat, Jesse retrieves a spiral sketchbook and a wand of colored chalk and follows the path of the two men through the shop's front room. Even in anger, especially in anger, a loving current runs between uncle and nephew; you can imagine a hard and lively smell like ozone. He notches several passes on the paper, trying to lock down the sweep of their connection. After a few minutes, Jesse closes the pad and watches Uncle D take center stage.

How different from his father's demeanor—the lean margins of his face, the eyes faintly blue. Louis Kerf, who patrols the aisles of his hardware store in a thin-lapelled suit that shows a trace of shine at knees and cuffs. Who chews each bit of dinner steak a minimum of twenty times. Who greets his customers by shaking hands, his son included, should he drop by.

A bellow swells out to the street, and the pizzeria's front door slams open. Dikran has Marty by a foot of braid; their four legs stagger toward the curb. "Get out of my store, you thief, goddamn you." His speech distends into a string of Armenian curses.

Marty has elected a Gandhi-like acquiescence and skids backward almost cheerfully, but when they near the car and Marty yanks himself free, Jesse detects the speed with which he drops his grin, the bitter crescents his clenched fingers dig into his palms. Marty drives away without looking back, in a state of composed and earnest reflection. For the first time in memory, his feet forget their restless dance upon the pedals.

They arrive at Jesse's class more than twenty minutes late. The studio doors are partway open and the instructor has brought one student to the fore to give her praise. A glimpse of her painting shows through onto the street, a starkly rendered head and body of a horse. "Don't bother stopping," Jesse says.

"You sure?"

"I don't want to make an entrance. Let's cruise."

Marty grins. "Sounds good. Sounds delicious. How about nowhere in particular—OK with you?"

They enter the turnpike heading west, pushing the Volvo far past its comfortable limits. The car's suspension bounces Jesse half an inch above his seat, but he hitches the back to its most suitable angle and settles in for the journey. Marty twirls one finger lightly on the wheel and scrounges in the glove compartment for his Ray-Bans and a candy bar. Voice thick with nougat, he points them toward the horizon and talks.

His subject is Uncle D's scar. One afternoon in 1917 the Turkish Army paid a visit to Dikran's village and rounded up most of the inhabitants and put them to the bayonet. Late in the night, his uncle came down from mountain pastureland

and found the corpses of his parents and his brother among a hundred others in the center of town. Laid out head to toe, D told him, like sticks of firewood.

Three uniformed stragglers were drinking coffee in the Balakian kitchen and they beat D with their hands and rifle butts, split the soles of his bare feet. His sister's photograph was on the mantelpiece—where was she hiding? For inspiration they laid his uncle face down on the floor, a bayonet against his neck. It made no difference—he wouldn't talk.

"He was fourteen," Marty says. "When I was a kid, he liked to show the scar when he was juiced on raki. Inch and a half long and red as a flare. Christ, that must have been something."

"What are you talking about?"

"That first moment, when the blood began to trickle down his neck—what was it, a couple of seconds? When he had to decide."

Ahead of them, the sun rides at tree level and light hits the glass in rapid, colorless bursts. Jesse has the airy sensation of being in perfect flight, of Marty guiding them solely by clarity of thought.

"Dikran thinks that I've been skimming," Marty says. "Doesn't matter what I say or how. He's got his temper, and he knows only what he knows—do not attempt to fix the vertical, do not attempt to fix the horizontal. I see it as a kind of primal beauty, especially at close range. The snake-brain acts without regard to reason."

They're going faster, ninety, ninety-five, and the Volvo's rattle intensifies, pitching octaves upward. Jesse braces a hand on the door. "You want to take it easy? You're making me nervous."

Marty yanks the wheel and they fishtail onto the berm, trees whipping by, gravel streaming against the hood. The landscape blurs. In his throat Jesse feels an exquisite bubble—they're going to spin, how strange, but Marty taps on the brakes and all they do is stall.

"That better?"

Jesse licks his lips, a rusty taste of dirt and bile. "You're out of your gourd, you know."

"Most likely."

Marty rolls the car back onto the highway and within a few moments, they are back at speed.

"Where now?" Jesse asks.

His friend's aviator lenses reflect a dark strip of road. "I say we stop when we hit California. My nickel."

"You're kidding."

"Dead serious. I'm curious about earthquakes, aren't you? The big ones, they say, the ground travels in a wave like ocean water. California, Jess. The Land of Sunshine."

Jesse reaches past his ankles for Marty's fallen Milky Way and holds it for inspection. "I've got one question," he says as he brushes off the dust.

"Yeah?"

"Were you skimming?"

Marty exhales thoughtfully. "Somewhat."

The candy is sticky from the heat of Jesse's hand, but sweet and comforting against his tongue. "Pull over," he says. "I want to drive."

SEVEN

THE DAY THEY ARRIVE IN SANTA CRUZ, Jesse waits at a beach south of downtown while Marty cruises off to check on a friend of a friend who might have a place where they can stay. Jesse has always been indifferent to the ocean, but standing by the edge of the Pacific he feels a hammering of affection and possibility. It may be the unfamiliar weather, a dry wind that eddies the sand and drifts a scent of redwood onto his body. He rolls up his blue jean cuffs and plants his heels against the rocking of the water. California—absolutely. Where these waves began their ride it is already tomorrow.

Up the coast there is an amusement park, and Jesse can pick out carousel music, a melody fractured by the wind as though the organist is drunk. The performance lays on a shabby welcome that makes Jesse laugh and strip off his sodden shirt and dive under the next waist-high roller. Spitting water, he lurches to the shore where he sits at the cool, wet boundary of the ocean.

Behind him he can hear the sound of two women settling in for an afternoon under the sun. Their subject is Watergate, which they dissect in energetic counterpoint. He could turn and have a peek, but even the most discreet rotation seems oversized and clumsy. Instead, he remains on the distant cloud line, following it to where the blues of sky and ocean are smoothly joined. He feels unalloyed contentment and a brilliant, sun-washed invisibility.

The soprano's fervor tilts toward outrage. The corrupt core of the Death Culture has been exposed; they should be making revolution, mobilizing the masses, taking it to the streets. She can feel it, Tricky Dick is going down. The alto responds with a modest laugh. Please, she says, the hearings are scripted top to bottom. Nothing's been exposed that both sides don't contract in advance. Short of a couple of tanks barrel first to the Oval Office, Nixon's going nowhere. She has a round, reliable delivery, a farm girl, Jesse imagines, accustomed to ringing in the hands for supper.

There is a pause in the conversation and Jesse switches position for a glimpse in their direction. The women are naked, one on her side, a blonde with a ripe, freckled bottom and a restless jitter along the limbs. The other lies carelessly upon her back, her face half-lost within the oval thrown by the brim of her sombrero. She is older than her friend, perhaps thirty. From instep to knee, her left leg wears a walking cast of rigid white. Jesse registers the immediate impression that she is staring at him.

As he watches in astonishment, she worms a wooden ruler between her cast and leg, pumping her elbow in a private fury of concentration, her brown hair flying. Well, Jesse thinks, naked—of course, isn't that the West Coast way? He yanks off his jeans, scouring his flesh with the salty denim. The women, when he turns again, are belly down. They pay no mind to him at all.

The sun has found a mean line to his pupils and Jesse flips onto his stomach, falling into drowsiness as though diving from a height. Before sleep comes, his last thought is of the twenty ladder rungs the brunette had to stump along to reach the sand.

The winds stall over Santa Cruz through late July, slamming windows shut and singeing the magnolia blossoms the color of burnt milk. There are fire warnings in the hills and the wail of sirens late at night. Jesse feels alive to the heat, as though it were inside of him and streaming outward.

He runs as often as he can—five bareheaded miles up King and Walnut and on through downtown trailing the morning traffic, saving his energy for the climb back to the Spanish-style house on Escalona Court he and Marty share with their three roommates. Some days, he runs to work, cruising to a stop inside the loading dock of Whole Earth Retreads, prickling with sweat and jetting his rapid breath into the dark warehouse. His shifts pass in a fog of hard labor. Seven hours of stacking eighty-pound cases of tire tread, his clothes stippled by a skim of melted rubber.

His work companions, lifers except for him, treat Jesse with a tiny measure of respect, call him College, or the Beast. It started once they saw him roll truck tires—one in each hand—up the loading ramp and pile them in the storage bays without excessive effort or complaint. There's a painting here, maybe, something lit by the glow of the extruder and livened by the spirited faces of the other guys. Dark faces, black rubber, shifting light from places where dirt has scraped away from the windowpanes. In the middle of Jesse's day, moments come when the pain in his back and arms leaves him, an instant when a truck tire is settling on the top of an eight-foot stack, when he is empty of who he is or what he's doing, when Jesse shakes free of the weight of his body, watching no one.

The house on Escalona was built in 1958 when Santa Cruz was colonized by military retirees and moneyed gentry from the Central Valley who parked their Fairlanes and Impalas underneath the eucalyptus trees. Jogging from his bus stop one September evening after work, Jesse slows down at his corner to enjoy the vista: the mild-toned terracotta roofs in rows against the hillside, the shell pink stucco walls, the early perfume of jasmine that will be overly sweet by dusk. Eyes closed, he could trace the scent and find his door.

Their house is the lone rental on the block and in the worst condition, marked by a patchy lawn and chipped paint and shunned by every neighbor but the dogs. At Marty's insistence, a piece of plywood Jesse painted has been nailed above the lintel. The smiling face of Uncle Ho. One day soon, Jesse thinks, he'll take it down to coat the man's beard with a brighter glaze of white.

In the living room, his housemate Paul watches cartoons while riffling through a well-pawed block of graph paper. In the blue-green backwash of the TV screen, Paul's round face gives off an accommodating aroma of marijuana and Dr Pepper. "Dig it," Paul says, raising his meaty fist in greeting. "So far I've clocked six minor assaults, three medium, one heavy, two deaths, and two resurrections. This motherfucker gets a slot in the permanent collection." He yells over his shoulder, "Nat, we got another keeper."

Under curling posters of Jack Lord and Che Guevara, Paul's girlfriend, Natalie, collates leaflets at the long dining table that all but fills the next room. Her expression is obscured by a tangled mass of blonde hair, though it seems to Jesse she slams down on her stapler with more authority than needed. Tomorrow night at the Civic Auditorium she'll lead a demonstration against the Miss California Pageant. She has no humor for the meandering fizz of Paul's intelligence.

Jesse never tires of watching her do the simplest things, as now she gathers mimeo paper and sorts by colored ink. Natalie wastes few movements; her actions condense into their leanest versions, even the quick, sisterly smile she lays out when she takes note of his attention. As usual she is wearing Danish clogs, which give her step a decisive, almost military clatter.

He steps to her side and lends a hand with the collation, careful to mimic Natalie's method, aware of her watchful eye. "Don't let me screw this up," he says. "Page two after page one, I got that right?"

Natalie wants to hide her laugh. "Appreciate the help," she says. "We've got hundreds of these to get on top of before tomorrow night. Once we get them sorted, it's staple and then triple fold."

"Triple fold," Jesse says. "When it comes to mindless effort, I think I'm going pro. Come and see me at the factory sometime. They call me Beast."

At this, Natalie winces a little. She's told him she's not sure a middle-class kid like him should be taking a job that could belong to a member of the working class. But help is help, and they work side by side happily enough. Is this what having an older sister is like? As an only child he can only guess. Someone to laugh at his jokes and keep him honest?

On the TV screen there's a hot jiggle of color and spastic energy, with a cat speeding on propeller legs over a cliff.

Paul's theory is that violence on kids' TV has tripled since the bombing of Cambodia fired up in 1970. He has a chart of the most lurid samples, plotted as to frequency, kinetic energy, and length. The parabolic curve the data make is like the shape of Nixon's nose, Paul says. He's undecided what to make of the connection.

"I think they had this on last month," says Jesse. "The cat gets flattened by a steamroller."

"Cliff fall, steamroller, fake tunnel, TNT kaboom, I'm gonna show it to my rats," Paul says. "They'll freak. The rat never lies."

Up at his UCSC lab, Paul shows five rats a daily dose of Warner Brothers animation, Chuck Jones, Tex Avery, and the like. Three months of immersion and the animals burn out the bearings on their treadmills. Six, they gnaw each other's tails. At eight, Paul sections through their hypothalami to analyze the sectors for aggression. Once Jesse asked him what he hoped his research might produce. No break in my allowance, Paul answered, with a grin composed of pride, contrition, and the better portion of a nickel bag of Humboldt Blue. Following that, OK, the downfall of the power structure as we know it.

Jesse finishes stapling Natalie's leaflets, then heads to the couch to watch cartoons, drinking cold Dr Peppers and smoking pot until the soundtrack starts to wriggle through his skull. He wanders onto the back porch where he checks his watch, his thoughts twirling loosely, and then there is a click from the neighboring yards on either side and automatic sprinklers switch on. He touches his dry tongue to his lips and catches the warm lick of mown grass.

At the far end of the driveway near the garage, Lucy hunkers over a set of wooden sawhorses. By the quantity of lumber at her side, she must be making protest placards for tomorrow. She stands barefoot, working quickly as the light recedes, her saber saw yowling through the cuts.

She is singing, Jesse marvels when she quiets her saw, an old mountain ballad of lovesickness and betrayed devotion. Her voice glides with tender feeling along the verse—until she turns and catches him listening. Silence moves between them as if by consent, and Lucy breaks into laughter and stamps on the asphalt, sending wood chips flying.

"Busted," she says between snorts. She fits her saw into its case and kicks it shut with her heel.

"I liked it. You have a sweet voice." Jesse lopes toward her, remembering at the last not to press too close. Lucy is five-two and often takes his height as a personal affront. "Your wicca's into Appalachian music, I guess. Or maybe a subset, you know, the pagan-lesbian-feminist-separatist-folk-singing subset." Jesse licks his lips again. "Did I mention I am completely stoned?"

"No shit." Lucy squats to fill her arms with boards. "How about shutting the fuck up and lending me a hand?"

"No problemo." Jesse boosts up a stack and straightens tremulously erect.

"I am not impressed." Lucy's pile is less than half as large.

"Biology is destiny, isn't that the line?"

"Don't push it." As she brushes past him, Jesse can see the white skin of Lucy's scalp. With her crew cut and cowlick, the button-front jeans she favors, she has the look of a fearless teenage boy. Her rep is legion for accelerating hearts at any number of Santa Cruz's lesbian bars.

"You gonna set that down," she asks, "or just space out on me?"

"Hmm. Multiple choice. Gimme a minute to see what I come up with."

Later while Lucy scrubs sap off her fingers at the kitchen sink, Jesse munches from a bag of granola. "Who's on dinner call tonight?" he wants to know.

Lucy jerks her head toward the wall the kitchen shares with Marty's bedroom. Through the plaster Jesse can detect a Mahler symphony at full throttle, and during a quiet passage, the daintier tempo of a woman's moaning.

"Ariel," says Lucy. "A Capricorn with Pisces rising. She told me on her way to the bathroom. She had one of those flowered zipper purses to stash her diaphragm. Pink daisies, man, just as sweet as you please. Her moon is in Jupiter."

"Meaning?"

"You wanna eat, you better cook. Myself, I have a meeting."

Jesse runs the faucet over his head. Under the icy water his neck tightens. His skin might sound a note if it were touched.

"Hey, Lucy, what you were singing, do you believe it? Love grows cold and fades away like the morning dew?"

Lucy flings her towel at Jesse's dripping face. "It's just a fucking song, Jesse. Mop up your mess, or somebody'll have your ass for breakfast."

Across the floor there is a muddy trail of Jesse's sneaker tracks. As soon as Lucy goes, he marches with purpose across the cracked linoleum, aiming for balance in the composition. "The water is wide—I cannot get over," he sings, evening the border with his tread. "And neither have I wings to fly."

EIGHT

THE KFAT MORNING SHOW is playing bluegrass as Marty coasts around the kitchen in his bathrobe. Drinking from a bottle of beer, he looks into a hand mirror to calculate the virtues of his changed appearance. Explosions of reflected light bob against his newly minted blonde curls.

At the counter, Jesse completes a set of stretches. Ten miles before breakfast—ten, goddamn it, and he might have done another five, the groove was that clean, his will that strong. At the center of the room, Marty scuffs aside dye-stained newspapers and slugs of shorn hair to perch upon a wicker stool.

"Okey-doke," he says, dipping the mirror in benison toward Ariel who hops forward. "Have at me."

Jesse turns to watch as Ariel leans her body into Marty's, nicking at his beard with a scissors, taming the point into a compact blond barb. She is wearing one of Marty's black T-shirts and white bikini underpants, and as she pauses to rough her fingers against Marty's sideburns, Jesse sees pink abrasions circling her wrists and ankles. Good God, Ariel shows qualities not instantly apparent. Marty's never mentioned that he has a taste for ropes.

In keeping with the women Marty often chooses, Ariel is eager-faced and young, with a bit of baby fat carried in her cheeks and chin. But she displays a tinge of secret knowledge—in her bitten lips, in the wild moss of armpit hair revealed by her loose sleeves. She poses Marty's face against her scissors in a stiff-fingered grip that raises impressions upon his flesh. He lets her move him how she likes.

Women appear in Marty's life without particular exertion on his part, and Jesse wonders how to learn the trick of his allure. "There's a fish," Marty explains one night. "A zippy Japanese item they call fugu. This item sets you back, I don't know, a hundred bucks a serving, depends on where the yen is with the market. Anyway, the liver is deadly—one bite will stop your clock in thirty seconds. The body flesh is worth so much because it's got a speck of neurotoxin nails your nervous system with a high hard one. The fingertips go numb and the tips of your ears, the heart scampers like a fucking poodle. The closer to the liver the chef slices, the more you pay, the more you risk, the more you feel.

"A little trouble and a reliable amount of nasty fun. A complexity in my attentions some women find invigorating to the spirit. That's my deal, and it works its charms. You, Little Brother, are just too goddamn nice. Roughen up and see what doors may open."

Blond, Marty seems happier than Jesse can recall. Only the mobile darkness of his eyes and the drop of his nose ring familiar. He hops off his stool and flicks hair from his bathrobe with a shimmy that exposes bare skin to his waist.

"Christ," Jesse says. "You even did your chest hair."

"That ain't all, pardner. Want a peek?"

"Spare me."

Marty has gained sight of himself in a mirrored picture frame and squirms to admire the view at several angles.

"You aiming for that messianic thing, I think you hit a bull's-eye," Jesse says.

"Don't say?"

"Absolutely. You look exactly like that swishy Jesus in the Pasolini movie."

Marty curls his fist to offer Jesse his middle finger. "Small is the gate and narrow the way," he says. "Know me by my sign."

Ariel steps between the two men. "I think Marty is beautiful. We picked the fawn tone to set against the flecks in his eyes. You have the grooviest eyes, did anybody ever tell you, love? You could dive right in."

Marty bares his canines toward Jesse. "Listen and learn. We California blonds, we have our depths." He pulls Ariel to him, allowing his fingers to fall against her small breast. "You delivered, babe. This is more than I hoped for. I feel—how to put it—sort of exalted."

Ariel cups Marty's hand with hers to halt the up-and-down of his thumb. "Gosh, I mean, a new hairstyle and all? Is your brother usually so serious, Jesse?"

Jesse looks to Marty, who shrugs with benign amusement. "We're both serious," Marty says. "Solemn as shit, handed the appropriate inducement."

"Runs in the family," Jesse says. "Blood will tell. Isn't that so, Big Brother?"

"God's truth," Marty says. His thumb renews its circular motion. This time Ariel accepts his caress.

The demonstration has an antic energy, like a late night party running out of kilter. Loudspeakers strung to a parked VW bus amplify a woman's singing through a squeal of electronic feedback. She sits on the van's roof, sailing prettily through a protest ballad, blowing kisses to the watchful cops between her stanzas. "Angry Young Dyke," her T-shirt reports.

Two hundred demonstrators mass the sidewalk by the auditorium where Miss California waits to earn her crown. Behind police barriers, on the Civic Plaza, there are four klieg lights whose beams speed starward in an outpouring of sound and light. In any given instant, Jesse reasons, the chanting, marching crowd might leap into stampede and he would follow. Or would if his high heels were not so wobbly.

He wears a chiffon frock of powder pink and pumps with satin bows to match the contest sash that's pinned from neck to hip. Natalie begged him into drag using sweet talk and revolutionary cant and a promise to do his dishes for a month. His orders are to win the notice of the press who prowl for footage on the plaza and the street. He serves his tidbit to the cameras with all the dignity his six-foot-two can bring to bear, a placard reading: MS. CONGENIALITY SEZ: SEXISM = RAPE.

As the demonstration goes on, Jesse locates an unexpected pleasure in the enthusiasm of the mob. Playing the fool, who would have thought? He adds a curtsy to his stroll and inclines his head to the whoops and cheers as though the affection were real.

On the opposite sidewalk, a woman watches the demonstration from the saddle of a bicycle. There is a familiarity to the jab of her foot against her pedal, to the spray of brown hair that feathers her neck. Then he sees the cast on her far leg, white as a tooth.

From the loudspeakers, the singer urges "love and freedom," and the woman launches through the crowd with verve and grace and aggression. Before she disappears around the corner, Jesse drops his sign and kicks his pumps into the gutter. He runs a hard canter, chasing the spark of her reflector and calling out to her to wait.

The woman pays no heed, stands upright upon her pedals, despite the cast, and notches along the Chestnut Street hill in a beautiful and resolute line. But Jesse closes the gap, and she stops and observes his uphill progress without so much as a smile. Perhaps she's seen her share today of barefoot men in party pink.

"You can't go that way," Jesse says in more panting fashion than he likes. "The governor's due any minute, and I personally know eight people who want to see how many eggs it takes to send the asshole back to Sacramento."

The woman sights up the tree-lined avenue of gingerbread Queen Annes only recently laced with drifting fog. "And how many do you think that would be? I expect Reagan's good for at least a dozen before he turns tail. Assuming he doesn't have his people open fire. Under the cover of arms, he'd go somewhat longer, wouldn't you guess?"

"I don't know. Maybe. I hadn't pictured gunplay."

The woman gives him her frank, open-faced regard. "I can always imagine the worst."

Her voice is much as he heard it at the beach, though more subdued than he recalls, as if the plaster weighs it down. Through the splay of her pants leg, cut to fit the cast, there is a morsel of tan thigh. Tan all over—the remembered image flushes through him. An untamed color like tree bark or sand.

"Do I know you?" she asks him. "I've seen you, I'm sure of it. I've got this memory for faces, pieces of faces and the like. It's a curse, believe me, sort of always having gravel in your shoe."

"What exactly do you remember?"

She dismounts to examine him at close reach. He smells her flowery perfume and an unnameable gamy funk.

"No," she says. "The chiffon throws me a curve. Sorry."

"The Forty-first Avenue Beach. The end of June."

Her smile has an agreeable limberness. "You bet. Your eyes. You checked me out, gave me your up and down and roundabout and pretended not to, I remember now."

The dress binds at Jesse's chest. "I don't think I did. I wouldn't." He fluffs his printed sash. "That would have been distinctly uncongenial."

She laughs. "It was a nude beach, hon. Everybody watches everybody—me included."

She introduces herself as Isabel Lantana and they sit at the curb, talking and watching the fog soften the prospect of houses, trees, and street. She works trimming hides for a used clothing and leather boutique called Rags to Riches; her scent derives from tannin and what she identifies as Condensed Cream of Cow. She lives alone in the Felton redwoods and chipped her metatarsal bone while doing limbo in a road-house out on Highway 9.

"I won grand prize," she says, skipping her fingers against her cast. "You're sitting beside top limbo dog of Santa Cruz County. I won a plastic trophy and a hundred dollars, not to mention a bottle of overproof rum."

"With a broken foot? In pain?"

Isabel is checking out the spot where Jesse claims the egg assault lies pending. "I needed new derailleurs for my bike," she says.

The fog is thickening around them and Jesse feels enclosed by it, untethered and calm, as though pleasantly lost at sea.

"Come now, walk me up the hill," says Isabel. "Maybe your friends will loan a girl an egg or two."

"You're sure? If something goes down, won't it be tough to get away?"

Isabel cushions her weight upon him to stand up, her hand callused and hot and strong. "We'll improvise," she says.

Her cast thumps on the sidewalk. Beside her, Jesse pushes the bike, scattering cedar bark and pebbles, feeling the beating of his heart like an engine in his chest.

NINE

L ET ME TELL YOU ABOUT ISABEL. Months went down before she nudged her luscious toes across our threshold. She drifted by as an idea. A name. A tale that Jesse told us over dinner. Nude On The Beach, The Limbo Dog, The Woman On Her Bicycle With Broken Foot. Jesse was ratcheted to higher levels than I'd ever witnessed, and played the parts in different voices. All fall he cooked up recipes that had a mighty zip and zing. I learned Bel first in his behavior before we ever met. The meals he served that season were addictive little wars. Chipotle chile moles, Jamaican jerk, treacly desserts that bounced an ache directly to the temples. The other roommates grumbled but I felt satisfied and grateful. I'd wipe my eyes and hail a toast up to the heavens. I like a dish that has the stuff to leave the mouth in shreds.

They loved to dance, that's what he told me. Met once a week on Fridays at a low-rent bar down by the pier. I knew the place, Lulu's, with its clientele of coke dealers and abalone divers, graybeard surfers at their tequila. The jukebox leaned toward Willie Colon and the Fania All-Stars. The air had the odor of kelp and, from its further reaches, a pleasant herbal dew.

I can see the two of them in their work clothes bumping through a frisky salsa. Behind them the bar talk rumbles on all night—the soured deals and sneaky ocean currents, the general capriciousness of Man and God and Nature. She leads and Jesse clings to all the dips and turns a half-step behind. Dancing with sentiment to the passionate Latin brass.

Friends, Jesse told me, that's what they decided. They'd start with conversation and shots of Sauza Gold and lime. She'd lick salt crumbs from the corner of her wrist and escort Jesse to the floor so that music and momentum could strip away her sense of where she was. They'd stay there hardly talking until she called the final number, then they'd chart their separate trails to separate beds.

But when are you gonna fuck her, was my point of view. Nothing wrong with good old Mr. Fuck. Even for friends. Especially for friends, if you pay attention to the details. Sex lends a merry fidget to a friendship, cranks it tight until it sits right up and begs. No telling what you'll get—messy sheets, or some intense species of disaster. Nothing from nothing—it takes a fleck of dirt to grow a pearl.

I'm happy, Jesse declared. We like our friendship as a partnership of equals—consider it an article of liberation that sex is off the table. He was facing away from me, but I caught the sweetest piece of fear flit through his vision. I made my mind up then to nose out Lulu's from a careful distance. I don't trust anybody's politics until I've seen them dance.

Isabel is sitting on a barstool waiting for merengue music when Jesse comes into the bar. It's the fast tunes she holds to, the swing and the frenzy, not these slow Celia Cruz heartbreakers full of untranslatable Cuban sorrow. He sequesters himself in the doorway as she finishes her drink. She strips a lime rind of its flesh with her teeth, double-snaps her shot glass to the bar and orders up another round.

She has on her favorite dancing outfit, a carnelian dress Jesse loves her in, scooped necked and featuring a print of snarling Chinese tigers. Their yellow bodies are sewn with rhinestones that thieve colored light from the electric beer signs on the facing wall. With no more thought than if she were alone, she twists her torso in a ballerina's stretch. Shimmers streak the rayon fangs and stripes and claws.

Work is caked over him, the char of overheated machinery, and Jesse jogs to the men's room for a session with the scrap of Lava he carries in his bag. He scrubs his arms and chest a stinging pink, steaming the mirror until he cannot see his face. Marching to the bar, he plants his still-damp fingers around Isabel's untouched glass.

Her look up at him is softened by alcohol. "You have soap in your ears," she says.

"It was a dirty day. You know how they are."

"Don't go feeling sorry for yourself. Dirt comes off."

Jesse swallows and sighs, and a cactus-flavored heat runs down his gullet. "God, what's finer than ending the week by drinking tequila on someone else's dime?"

Isabel motions to the bartender for two more. "Nothing I can think of," she says. "Next round's yours."

They drink while Isabel unrolls the story of her week—a history of missed deadlines and bicycle flats and bounced checks and lost earrings. "My life's turned into slapstick," she says, with a note of amusement and pride. "It's a lesson, I have to think, a past life sniffing at my heels. But I don't intend to let it spoil the evening. Good behavior only. I'm aiming upward."

"I like it. Upward. Do you have any idea of how great you are?"

"You're being foolish."

"No, I'm not," Jesse says. He crowds closer to her, smelling citrus and the musk he knows her by. "Here you are, even after a miserable patch like this—you're barely mussed. You don't even know how to complain."

"Is someone going to come and save me if I do?"

"Not the point. Nothing's out of place, don't you see? You have your house in the woods, a job you don't exactly hate, a dancing partner who'll last the night. Tranquility reigns. We're aiming upward."

Isabel shakes her head in wonderment. "Connect the dots and there I am."

"I was trying to make you feel better. Not put you in a box."

"Yet here I am."

She isn't beautiful—not in the school-taught, classical sense. Her features are too peasant-shaped; her appetites and scars and hungers range in the open—an image out of Goya or Millet. Jesse collars her within a sidelong stare. Her dusk-colored eyes hide a terrain of undeclared emotion.

The jukebox has switched over to a Portuguese vocal of exquisite soulfulness and the singer's moody phrasing brings Isabel up short. "I don't understand what kind of downer Lulu's on," she says. "It's Friday night, for heaven's sake. Mambo, mambo, mambo, don't you think?"

Jesse rises unsteadily to his feet, feeling the peculiar surprise of too much drink. "I hope the old woman's in a friendly frame of mind. If I'm not back in twenty minutes call the shore patrol."

In spite of herself, Isabel sways to the melody. "It means fate," she says.

"I'm sorry. You've lost me there."

"Fado. This kind of song."

He waits for further elaboration. "Go on," Isabel says, shooing him off, smiling her covert smile. "I want my workout."

In her office near the fire exit, Lulu sits before a plate of Moros y Cristianos. She stalls Jesse in attendance on her couch, audience to the clatter of the bangles on her wrists. The bar owner takes her rice and beans indolently, enjoying Jesse's impatience as though it were an extra course. At last, freshening her lipstick and straightening her enormous dress, she leads him to the Wurlitzer where he hurries to pick out tunes to flood the dance floor with their heat.

"Mira," Jesse hears Lulu's syrupy voice behind him. "You have the right heart you can dance to anything you like."

In a far corner, Isabel revolves to the fado in a slow, lightly held samba. There is no mistaking her companion's bleached hair or the pressed, white guayabera shirt, which Jesse recognizes as his own. Marty puts Isabel through a turn and twirls her in reverse, rustling her skirt around her calves. A second effortless twirl. Isabel's laughter soars loose above the sounds of singer and guitar.

Lulu breathes onion against Jesse's cheek. "He's a strong dancer, that one." In her musical accent, the old woman's words fuse with the Portuguese lyrics; she might be murmuring the chorus.

"Yes," he says finally. "He's got some moves."

"And you know him? He is your friend?"

Jesse concentrates on the dancing couple. Their bodies are

spotted with a pelt of mirror-ball illumination. "They both are," he says. "My two best friends."

"Ah," Lulu says, cocking her gaze toward the pair.

Jesse crouches over the jukebox. "Help me, Lulu. Which merengue do you love the most? Which makes you feel like you're back home in Santo Domingo?"

Her song arrives in a brilliant salvo of horns and congas, a rhythm section like a howling jungle. Johnny Ventura, she tells him, the king of them all. Across the room, Isabel holds out her arms for Marty's taking. Before the verse is over, they are indistinct among a flock of dancers who have rushed the floor. Jesse puts himself near to the speakers, where the music has a weight like a constant, thumping wind. From this vantage the postures of the merengue seem formal and showy, but Isabel and Marty attack them with a carefree spirit. As they swirl now and again into sight, they wave to Jesse with unforced affection, pleased to show off their fanciest maneuvers to their friend. Marty is moving his lips, Jesse sees, so as not to lose the complicated meter of the steps.

TEN

WHOLE EARTH RETREADS FILLS A BLOCK in the railway district west of downtown, two stories of sallow pre-war stucco. In a fit of architectural enthusiasm, the building's designer hitched a facade of Mission tiles to the edge of the flat warehouse roof and inset arches above the second-story windows. Our Lady of the Lug Nut, Jesse calls the place—where tires are born to life anew.

He does his time in the dark holds of semi-trailers, heaving worn-out truck tires to the warehouse floor at more than sixty pounds a throw. They land with a violent, rubbery boom, inflaming his nostrils with a scat of soot and truck exhaust. He's never felt so tired or so filthy or so strong.

His partner Henry Johnson wears a truss over green work pants and carries in his breast pocket a large bottle of Louisiana Hot Sauce, which he splashes against his tongue as the afternoon wears long. He exceeds Jesse's quota with an elegant minimum of exertion, all middle-aged hip and finesse. In Henry's thinking, Jesse wastes too much muscle on his day.

"You have some size, College, I give you, but your working habits are puny. Time is short and money's funny. Johnson's Rule is always do the boss a little shy of what he wants to earn your green."

At noon break, Henry and the other men take stations at the factory windows, playing grab-ass and chomping hot link poor boys and tamales they've reheated on the tread extruder. Through the open transoms they shout to women on the sidewalk, cheering at the catcalls that fly upward in return. As newest hire, Jesse stands guard behind a barrier of rubber-speckled shirt backs, satisfied with a narrow slice of gray November sky. How will he handle it, he wonders, if the men rain their attention on a woman that he knows—Lucy, perhaps, or Isabel?

Lucy would find a rock and flash it to the windows, star the glass, he's sure. But Isabel? She'd pedal by Our Lady full speed, tires hissing on the pavement, eyes on the road ahead. The only difference between men and dogs, she's told him more than once—dogs can be trained.

"What about Top Limbo Dogs?" Jesse had asked. This was amid the wreckage of breakfast in the Escalona dining room a week after Isabel and Marty met.

She sipped the last of her tea with a modest dipping of her chin. "They're an exception. They can't be taught a thing." Her hair was wet from the shower and hung weedily against her neck. From the kitchen they heard Marty doing dishes, and Isabel smiled so sweetly at the racket, Jesse wanted to look away. Marty was singing Sonny Boy Williamson and splashing holy hell inside the sink.

The Whole Earth whistle signals end of lunch, and Henry pushes from his window perch. "I had seventy-five dollars," he says, "I'd buy some halter tops at Pick 'n Save and hand them out like Mister Johnny Appleseed. I'll be fair-minded, any pretty young sister I happen to meet, black, white, or polka-dotted. Get one of those folding chairs and maybe a pint of V.O. and choose a watching spot nearby the walking mall. Won't it be fine to let the world go bobbing by."

"You're a man of charitable instincts," Jesse says.

"I am well organized, son. All I need is capital."

"Come summer if you're short, I'll be your banker, we'll go fifty-fifty."

"Come summer, shoot, you'll be long gone. But I appreciate the offer very kindly."

"Where'm I going to be?"

Henry spikes a ruby assault of Tabasco into his mouth, sprinkling the space between them with vinegar and pepper. "Back where you belong, I expect." He hitches up his truss and lumbers past Jesse, offering high-five to every buddy on the line. A fanfare of slapping palms steers Henry back to work.

The shift boss is a twenty-two-year-old named Mitchell Michaelson Jr., the firstborn of the factory owner. Little Mitch has a way of wandering his attention around the compass when he talks. His floury complexion, Henry claims, is a proven tell of a devoted whack-off artist. Of late, he's taken an unfortunate liking to Jesse, corners him at lunchtime several times a week to spitball marketing concoctions—blimps and banners, a retread exposition at the County Fair. He speaks about the Whole Earth Family of Products with the deferential whisper of a golf announcer waiting for a putt.

Today, as Jesse rounds the corner toward the loading bay, Michaelson is shambling by in a corduroy suit, trawling the warehouse lanes for malingerers and thieves. His wan face gleams dangerously with good news.

"Hi there, Jesse. I know something about you."

"Yeah, what might that be?" Behind the boss, Henry grunts as he piles cold-cure rubber onto a pallet.

"Donelle Bishop just got fired," Little Mitch says.

"The order clerk? I don't think I've talked to her three times since June."

"Chick punched her sister's time card out last night—that's fraud, I guess. Big Mitch canned her at lunch. The sister, too. They're lucky Dad's too soft to prosecute."

"Maybe Donelle should have punched out Big Mitch instead."

"Ha. Ha. So, here's what, I told Big Mitch you probably type OK, you've been to college, you're good people. We're giving you your opportunity." His look grazes Jesse's ponytail. "You'll have to cut that mess."

"You want me for Donelle's job?"

"Well, yeah, sure. We're bumping you $37.25 a week, I think. Better a bump than a poke with a pointed object, ha ha."

Little Mitch's mouth jerks into a smile and then his attention latches onto the extruding equipment, which groans as though the machinery were working up an effort.

"I'd like to think it over, Mitch," Jesse says. "I've just figured out which end is up here on the floor."

The boss's Adam's apple throbs. "Think it over—jeez. My dad will burst a vessel, I told him you'd be golden."

In the trailer Jesse can see Henry shadowed by a pile of Michelin steel belts. The older man swabs the flat of his neck with a handkerchief, folds it slowly into a beautiful, lustrous square. "I'll give it serious consideration," Jesse says, moving past Little Mitch toward the dock. "Weigh all the pros and cons."

"Maybe you can keep the hair if you promise to comb it nice," Little Mitch calls out.

"I'll think it over."

Jesse pulls onto the trailer bed beside Henry and squats to launch his first tire of the afternoon. He pauses, straightens up, and leans it gently off his body to the ground. Golden, he thinks. What would that feel like?

On Fridays in my trusty Volvo, we rattled across the county from Boulder Creek to Watsonville, me and Isabel and Jesse, searching out dinners in the lowliest corners we could find, on the hunt for what was difficult or strange. In Half Moon Bay there was a Greek who roasted lamb tongues over grapevine twigs, sweet as candy, and one time in Capitola, we came upon a Navy SEAL named Huey Huge, large-size hombre who farmed sea urchins from pilings he seeded near the pier. We bundled up in blankets and convened by the water's edge, gooey roe on sourdough ficelle. We ate while I recited the Balakian family history—our wealthy century of feuds and larcenies, our hundred thwarted loves. The urchin dinner made fine company for that extravaganza—a briny taste of tears and sex, a husk whose spines will shoot you to the trauma ward, you don't look closely to your footing.

Afterward, we'd tool up Highway 9, the three of us snug in the front, radio playing Rollins or Dolphy or Miles. I'd drive and Jesse'd sing out for turns and fallen scrub, while in between us, Isabel head-bopped with the solos, blood-warm and happy. The road bucked us through the fog but we slipped along with confidence as though tacking through the chop. Home in one piece every time.

Jesse loved her. Who wouldn't—her face transported by the music, her eyelids bruised by all the Southern Comfort she'd been nursing. The sweetness of oranges when she kissed you good night. He loved her, Christ, he doted on us both, but without a sign of resentment he gave us room to be what we were, do how we did.

She loved him, too. Him more than me, I did the math the day we danced at Lulu's. He might have given her a try—it would have bent me nicely out of shape, instructed me to mind my manners. They never took the dare, not then. Too bad. If property is robbery—and that was how we understood it in those times—then in my thinking, same's fair for lovers.

The letter from his dad lies unopened on top of the television where Jesse dropped it earlier in the week. It's addressed in pencil in the seemly engineer's script his father learned at trade school. Written after dinner, Jesse decides—pot roast, frozen peas with margarine, one scoop of lemon sherbet, a Lorna Doone. Written at Jesse's student desk, in Jesse's one-time bedroom, Dad twirling a mechanical pencil under the virginal light of Jesse's gooseneck lamp. Here, in dependable monthly installments, Louis Kerf writes letters on Kerf and Co. stationery. Their arguments are as orderly as a toolbox.

It's thrilling to watch the man who once described a fine arts diploma as $20,000 toilet paper plead for Jesse to trot home to the studios on Huntington Avenue. There's a world of boundless possibilities when the Hardware King of Somerville becomes dismayed because his boy has lost the urge to paint.

Except he hasn't. At night, staring into his bedroom mirror, Jesse has been at it with a box of Conté crayons, six colors—earth tones, grays, and blacks. Hard to say why it's only self-portraits, but he's been nudging this along for several months, committed to finishing one a day. The more Jesse works, the more the series has abstracted, and now it's hard to say if anyone could recognize his latest as his face—or any face at all. He's shown the drawings to no one, stashing them under his bed when done. All he cares about is the gesture—the movement of his fingers across seventy-pound vellum, the smudge of his tortillon against the page, the smell of fixative that settles over bedclothes, pants, and floor. Momentum is what counts, more than vision, more than imagination. Making paintings like rolling tires up a ramp.

One evening in early November, Jesse waits on the front porch for Isabel and Marty, who's scored them tickets to a sold-out concert by the Who. It's been raining for a week and Escalona Court is shiny with runoff. Even boxed in under dense clouds, the Bermuda grass and jade plants smack the retina with an amazing green. So many separate greens: Coke bottles and dollar bills, the tarnished copper of a Revere Ware pan. At the bottom of the grade, he makes out Marty's Volvo surging up the hill. Coffee-colored water spits behind its wheels. The California palette: color rampant. Landscapes next, he thinks, more colors, too.

Jesse bolts into the downpour flapping his arms and hollering out a lunatic hello. The car swerves and collects him and they slalom up the hill toward San Francisco, his friends welcoming him with Marty's Afghan hash and Isabel's Jim Beam. Jesse draws in on the pipe and spends out the smoke with a shuddering laugh that whirls water from his matted head. "Faster," he orders Marty. "I don't want to miss a note."

"Lord, you're a total wreck," says Isabel. She slips out of her jacket and cloaks it around his shoulders. "Not me," Jesse says, watching the rain burst against the windshield. "Couldn't be better. Not if I tried."

The Who's performance is a vital substance flung up from drums and laser lights and Peter Townshend's windmill arm on his guitar. The volume is so profound, so large, it hauls the audience forward as if by pull of gravitation. Near the apron—or as near to it as the uniformed security will allow—dancers swarm to the music: an organism of jouncing limbs and Bic lighters propped overhead in communion with the band. If he closes his eyes, Jesse can feel the rhythms inhabiting the spongy cavern of his brain. A vertiginous sensation, as though he's been inflated to the point of flight.

Marty has brought them to the special real estate in sniffing distance of the stage. There was magic, Jesse recalls, how Marty worked his number in the parking lot before the show—converting their general-entry tickets into fifteen hits of acid, then acid into a rack of Day-Glo Frisbees, and Frisbees into press credentials, which greased them to the velvet-roped enclosure at the front. He snapped their passes gaily underneath the ticket-taker's nose. He's spent his concert climbing back and forth to the top bleacher rows in the rear, preferring the spectacle from above, he claims, but Jesse figures likely financing next week with the remainder of his stash.

Isabel stands next to Jesse, hands on her hips, chin jutting toward the performance in a posture of sulky appreciation. The Who's variety of muscle lacks the feints and subtleties of the Latins she loves, yet when Roger Daltrey slides to his knees near the proscenium's edge and lassos his microphone around his head in a flash of glinting light, she unleashes herself at last. In one of her wilder spins, her elbow creases Jesse across the ribs.

"Give her some room," Marty comes over to yell in Jesse's ear. "Once she cuts loose, Bel doesn't know her strength."

"I'll tough it out," Jesse shouts back. "She's having fun."

"Ain't we all. We're in the fucking United States of Fun."

There is a pause in the music, and the band retires in conference behind the banks of amplifiers stage rear. Isabel drinks from her pint bottle, glossy with the satisfactions of physical movement. She listens with Jesse while Marty ranks this concert against the one he saw at Suffolk Downs when he still lived in Massachusetts. There's a catch in his voice, a stutter in the larynx, which might be psychedelics coming on—the mescaline that Marty likes is often cut with speed. To please his lady-love, Marty has shaved his beard and cropped his dyed-blond hair back to its roots. Below the grizzled forehead, his pupils dilate, a canny and opalescent black.

"You never said you were planning to trip tonight," Jesse says.

"A few mics floated my way. You want?"

Jesse attempts to focus on his watch—fourteen hours will plunk him in the belly of tomorrow afternoon. "I better not. Happy trails, though."

Marty shakes his head mournfully. "Listen to him, Bel: 'I better not.' The working hump's lament."

"Most of us have jobs," Isabel says. She tucks her fingers within the crook of Jesse's arm. "I'd hate to think of him tripping at the factory."

"Cool," Marty says. A grin trembles across his face. "Always another day."

"It's not so bad," Jesse finds it necessary to insist. "Anyhow, I'm truly ripped behind your hash. How can I put it—less is more."

Marty pinches Jesse on the cheek. "Little Brother, less isn't more. More is more." He lunges off into the crowd, parting the bodies before him as though striding through the corn.

There is a lengthy stall waiting for the concert to resume, and a party atmosphere ping-pongs from wall to wall, echoing war whoops and, after a while, clapping in building unison. Isabel's face flushes in drunken yearning as she applauds and stamps and cheers.

The picture comes to Jesse of one of Paul's cartoon kitty-cats tumbling past a cliff—its optimistic smile as it bicycles its legs midair to stay aloft. Under Jesse's sneakers, the parquet quakes and shifts, raising a mucky scent of mud and dope and dancers' sweat. Hope, Jesse thinks, joining his stamping to the rest. We live in the expectation of a kind and boundless future.

In a burst of sonic thrust, the Who return to center stage. Pete Townshend announces that Keith Moon's gone off ill, he's dosed himself on veterinary medication, he can't stay upright on his drummer's stool. To take them through the last two songs, they've found a volunteer whose chops aren't halfway bad, a ballsy sod who promises the stuff to make it with the Who.

A spotlight paints the drum kit pearly white. It's Marty— has to be—drumsticks spread high for the downbeat, his knobby skull flashing scarlet and emerald green from spinning side-stage fixtures. Impossibly at home behind the drums. He scowls gravely, and at the cut of Pete Townshend's strumming arm, lays on the attack. He wields a competent, simple, aggressive hand during the first two numbers, and if he falters a bit with the complexities of the finale, the Who don't seem to mind.

Isabel pounds on Jesse's back, straining to see over the taller heads in front, so he hoists her onto his shoulders where she remains through the bravos and the bows. She is sturdier than he imagined, heels dug into him and waving her arms, more than once close to toppling them down. After the closing curtsies, Marty dogs the band into the wings.

In the parking lot, Jesse tries to find a route past the hired muscle who bar the backstage door. They have the surly appearance of schoolyard bullies; it will take all the bravado he can muster. The rain has ended, leaving a chill transparency in the night sky. Radiational cooling, he remembers from a class he took at Northeastern. Nothing to bind the warm clouds to the earth.

Isabel will wait by Marty's car. She tells Jesse, "Enjoy yourself to your heart's delight for half an hour. If you're not back by then, I'm thumbing home."

"I can't believe you're passing up a party with the Who."

She indulges him with a goodbye kiss. "If there's anywhere a girlfriend is extra weight, it's got to be a party with the Who."

He watches her departure through the line of traffic, a skipping quality to her step as though she still hears music.

When Jesse returns to the Volvo, Isabel is bent atop the pavement in the Warrior yoga pose. "You're limping," she says and comes to him with an instinct to push her touch on every hurt: his torn shirt pocket, a banged-up knee, three scratches on his face. "They beat you up, those creeps."

"Just shoved. I was urged to stay outside. I'll tell my grandkids I got my ass thumped by the henchmen of the Who. I'm not unhappy."

Isabel stares past him toward the Cow Palace, where the exterior lights are clicking off. "He's going to be impossible, you know," she says. "We'll be listening to his folderol till Christmas."

"He's earned the right. I don't believe his luck, can you? To be there when they were choosing drummers."

"I didn't know he played that well," she says.

Jesse dusts his pant legs and gravel showers the ground in a lively clatter. "Hey, I never knew he played at all."

Isabel yawns. "Okey-doke," she says. "Let's book, if you don't mind. Marty's probably warming himself with a teeny-bopper from the band's collection. His new friends can worry how to get him home."

"We don't have any car keys," Jesse tells her, but Isabel worms her arm through the front vent window. Grunting, she pops the lock and slides on her back under the dash. The engine warbles into life.

"Wow," Jesse says.

Isabel touches two fingers to her brow. "I'm lucky, too," she says. "Keeping me company?"

Along the Felton Highway switchbacks, the headlamps ghost light against the redwoods, tree trunks vanishing almost as rapidly as they appear.

"It doesn't make you mad?" Jesse says.

"What's that?"

"About Marty and whoever, his teeny-bopper for the night?"

Her expression recedes into the general darkness.

"Might as well get mad about the weather," Isabel says.

ELEVEN

AFTER EIGHT DAYS OF INCOMMUNICADO Marty surfaces at Escalona House before daybreak, a Sunday morning. There's a howling from the shrubbery, a pounding on the latched front door that herds Jesse out of bed and down the stairs. It's a gusty morning, mule-gray with fog, yet on the doorstep Marty is barefoot and dressed in a Hawaiian shirt and matching shorts in tones that call to Jesse of the cherries in a drink at Trader Vic's. His friend's blinking, sun-chapped face sways beneath a bright Panama hat.

"Hi-de-ho, Little Brother, Salaam Alaikum."

"You know what time it is?"

"Don't fuss."

He bumps past Jesse in a vapor of beer and what might be suntan lotion past its prime. In the living room, Marty trails his fingers on what he passes: stereo speakers, the construction spool he and Jesse liberated from a U.C. building site, some Santa Cruz Whole Women's Catalogs that Natalie is hawking from a kiosk up on campus.

"Plus ça change," Marty says. He widens his arms into a loving O. "Give Daddy a squeeze. It's great to be home."

Jesse shakes his head. "No thank you. When was the last time you had a shower?"

"Ah," Marty says. "It hasn't been a shower kind of week."

"No? I kind of pictured you sharing a bathtub with a pair of groupies like Mick Jagger did in *Performance*."

Marty falls on the couch, spreading out against the corduroy with an elaborate groan. "Expand your imagination," he says, and knocks his hat brim over his eyes. After a bit he snores. His slumber is a mixture of athletic snorts and contortions. Dreams, Jesse guesses. What dust does traveling with the Who kick up into the subconscious?

Outside, the fog is lifting and the sky is colored by an insistent wash of wintry blue. It's a day for running distance, Jesse decides—the wind ramming on his back, pushing him faster than he can do on his own.

The weak sunshine shafts into the room. Lord, Marty's body is streaked with party glitter, patches of it twinkling from his instep to his knees. His friend squirms in sleep. The specks toss up a multicolored mess into the air.

At Sunday breakfast I told the Escalona roommates about my week out on the road. We were in the kitchen eating pancakes. Perfect silver dollars. I was flipping them directly from the pan onto the plates. The action's in the wrist—a little confidence, they goddamn sail.

I was bug-eyed with exhaustion and semi-drunk on Bloody Marys, but I loved how my subject bopped along my tongue. Life with the band. You should have been there— the smell of scorching butter, Jesse and the others bouncing round the stove like kittens after cream. We were eating with our fingers, licking syrup off our skin.

God is in the details, so the man says. The quantities of what was snorted, dropped, or smoked; the sundry contortions of the rock stars and their pals. Natalie, the true believer, built up a Marxist thesis: that rock-and-roll is agitprop and nurtures solidarity among the working class. Roger Daltrey's skinny body got her wet, I'd wager cash.

How it flowed, my little drama. First we boogied on a tour bus from the Cow Palace to concert dates in Isla Vista and L.A. and San Diego. I made myself essential to the band as Keith Moon's backstage keeper. I was the tender shepherd of his stash. Doled out downs and ups and joints and shots of frozen Stoli. I logged the calculus on whether Moon could take the freight.

Keith was a motherfucking superman of impulse. Shy sort who'd toss a hotel TV set eleven stories to the swimming pool to watch it splash. No matter what complexity of chemicals the dude absorbed—and let me say, he was prodigious—he'd drive the music in a rigid fury every night as if the tunes were masonry he had to smash. I kept him vertical, drumsticks wailing. I knew my place. I merited my keep.

After the San Diego gig, the band took R & R in Ensenada where we lunched on marlin tacos at Hussong's bar. We slugged mescal from the bottle, we lost pesos by the thousands at the jai alai fronton up in Tijuana. The pelota hits the wall at 180 miles an hour, it's in the Guinness Book of Records, did you know?

This was lush territory, the Brits and me in Baja, until Isabel came in the kitchen. She'd biked the fourteen miles from Felton and her face exuded virtuous pink effort. There was a blood-red ribbon tying up her braid, as I recall. I should have hustled her away for a private greeting, but I was liquored up and Paul was taking notes; I couldn't stop.

Night before last the band and I swam alongside leaping dolphins in the Gulf of California. The waves were veined with glowing plankton, we were terrified about the things that might come chomping up at us from underneath. There's nothing quite like porpoise love, their blunt, brutal adoration. If they could appreciate what animals we humans truly were, they'd drown us all in twenty seconds flat.

Isabel seemed charmed and favored me with an admiring look. She whispered into Lucy's ear, which goosed a grin across her face. I lost my footing there, went dry. I'd been shading the truth from the outset, hatched my story out of air, one sentence at a time. My friends, I thought, would have me pegged in half a second. I never would have guessed they'd be so easily misled.

You're not surprised, are you? The actual events were nothing to advertise—Wham Bam Thank-You Ma'am in the dressing room while the final encore was still banging in my head. Facts are dependably small and lacking in kindness, don't you think? They lead us only where we suspect they're going to. Where's the lift in that?

I took a breath, the sour iron of fatigue and hangover. Then I confessed. Turned on a dime, if you want to know, made myself dizzy. There was a van of surfer dudes from Malibu who stopped for me on PCH. I crashed at their party shack on Zuma Beach in the shadow of the cliffs where Charlton Heston barebacked his horse in *Planet of the Apes*. They were growing sinsemilla in their closet, and I helped them sex the plants. The money's in the female buds. The rest is trash.

Jesse's eyes were liquid, his smile had boiled down into a chalky line. Isabel was fidgeting against the kitchen counter and I wondered if she planned to bolt. God, she was beautiful then, frisky with uncertainty. I can't remember when I loved her more.

She pushed herself from her ledge, came to me in a few bold steps, her dancer's glissade. Her arms crept around me, her lips were spidery against my neck. And then her fingers prowled beneath the open collar of my shirt. Before I saw what she was after, she'd yanked a handful of my chest hairs out by the roots.

A jolt flamed through me, tears welled. Isabel was dazzling, absolutely pure in her anger. The roommates were laughing and I tipped my straw fedora, took my bows. "Welcome home, Marty," I remember Isabel saying. "All your bullshit perked up my appetite. If you've got any batter in the bowl, I'd like a short stack, please, and let's go heavy on the syrup."

We were all right after that. Back on track, and for a good long while, better than before.

That evening Marty decamps with his belongings to Isabel's cottage, where he remains out of sight until New Year's. From time to time his leavings wash up at Escalona House like the residue of a mysterious civilization. A bushel bag of baby artichokes, a pair of orange freeway hazard cones, a carton of T-shirts honoring the Comet Kahoutek, an envelope of Deutschmarks equal to Marty's share of two months' rent. Jesse plays organizer, dividing out what the roommates want and chucking everything else into Marty's abandoned room.

It becomes Jesse's custom to visit Lulu's after Friday supper. From the bar he watches the dancers and sips a Red Stripe beer. Lulu urges partners on him, finding women who are twice his age and who smell of rum and lipstick. For a samba or two, Jesse sways with them beneath the spinning mirror ball. Their thighs, encased in pantyhose, wedge into his crotch; their cocktail rings dig against his fingers when he shakes their hands goodnight.

He and Paul devote their Saturday afternoons to the Million Dollar Movie on channel eleven, auditioning candidates for Paul's new treatment on his rats. Paul's interest has moved from cartoons onto films. According to him, cinematic images have infused a new order of fears into the American psyche. The deadliest are those in black-and-white, the color of dreams.

Staring at the TV, notebooks in hand, the two roommates catalog lava eruptions and deep-sea diver drownings, pyramid entombments and monster attacks. Paul's favorites are period drama beheadings where the screen goes blank at the moment of impact.

"It's all about control," Paul says. "What they show you and what they won't. There's the ax, see, and the thud and the black screen. That black is something very groovy, believe me. I gotta see how my little guys up at the lab respond. I bet they'll do the hokey pokey over a guillotine. Spike my graphs up to the roof."

Natalie walks behind them toward the kitchen. She lugs a box of vegetables from the food co-op, and Jesse feels the urge to sit up straighter, as if he's been caught doing something he shouldn't. "Do they have feelings, your rats?" he asks Paul.

"Fear and hunger. They get depressed if you fuck with them enough." Paul stares at Jesse, fingers tapping on his lips as though he's working his mind around a problem.

"What?" says Jesse. "You're weirding me out."

"I'm thinking about Christmas," Paul says. "Going to see your ma and pa?"

"Not this year," Jesse says. "I had to convince them not to fly out here. I'm solo, which is fine."

"So you got nothing on the books? Wild."

"The factory is on vacation. I'm hanging out and looking for trouble."

Paul straddles the couch arm and tells Jesse about a psych department associate who is desperate for subjects for her master's thesis project. His face blooms with scientific zeal. "It'll be a gas, you get to be a footnote."

"Doing what?"

"She's keeping it super hush. Gotta be something in b-mod, this chick graded term papers for B.F. Skinner at Harvard when she did undergrad."

Natalie has overheard the conversation and comes over to the couch, plunks herself between them. "We can do Christmas here, guys. Or Hanukkah, or something else, solstice, maybe. Nobody has to go solo. Isn't that why we choose to live together? Solidarity?"

Paul's grin tightens into an unhappy line. The muscles of his jaw are working hard, his inner monologue made flesh. Paul is not an arguer, though, especially not with the love of his life. Jesse waits to see which way things break. But Paul is silent, Natalie's hand on his knee as a reminder of what she wants. December has been almost constant rain and the gray light flickers through the living room window, populating the TV picture with undulating shadows. The only sound in the house is the lush Franz Waxman movie score.

"Give me your psych friend's number," Jesse says to Paul. "I'll call her tonight." He turns to Natalie. "Wonderful idea, solidarity. Love you for it, Nat. You cool if I beg off? My favorite holiday is None of the Above. A psych experiment sounds just my kind of weird."

She offers him a tiny sigh. "Your call, do what you will."

"Trying to," Jesse says. "It's why I'm signing up for Paul's friend's thing. My behavior could use some modification."

TWELVE

THE EXPERIMENT IS SET FOR THE EMPTY DAYS between Christmas and New Year's. Paul's friend coordinates by telephone, limiting her conversation to details of time and location. Her goal is to explore the effect of solitude on short-term memory. For the sake of anonymity, Jesse's label will be Subject Blue. A good choice, Jesse decides, a name of particular moods and textures. "I'll jump to anything you want," he says. "But what do I call *you*?"

"We won't be meeting. You're not hanging me out to dry, are you? I gotta have people I can depend on, otherwise fuck it." New York, he decides, the union of hostility and need.

"I'm your guy," Jesse says.

On December 27, the S.C. grounds are deserted. In solitude, the whitewash of the campus buildings, the tended paths of redwood mulch advance the hasty cheerfulness of newly built shopping centers and apartment complexes. At the highest point on campus, Jesse peers out over the distant harbor, the water churned by weeks of rain into a quilt of clay-brown swell and foam. Where head shops and burrito parlors jam the Beach Boardwalk, Spanish pirates once moored their boats to count their spoils.

For the next five days, Jesse inhabits a windowless basement room within the Psych Department complex in College V. There is a contract to sign before the experiment begins: no visitors, no phone calls, no unscheduled bathroom breaks, no personal belongings. The list goes on for more than a page. "Want it in blood?" Jesse asks the undergrad who logs him in.

"No talking to the monitors without permission," the student says. "I have to mark you off for this."

"I hear you," Jesse says. "My God is an angry God. Far out." He pens his signature without reading to the end.

The plan requires him to study out-of-order chapters selected from the King James Bible. Eight times a day he takes a test of fifty questions on each section, then slips his papers to a grader through a mail slot in the door. Surely the chapters have been chosen for their stony prose—a wilderness of begats and ancient place-names and the titles of kings and prophets.

By the end of the first session, his oxygen feels stepped on by mimeo fumes and the pallid after-bite of his TV dinner. Stretched out on his army cot, Jesse waits for someone outside his door to dim the overhead lights. The brilliance presses through his eyelids like a thumb. Irad begat Mehujael. Mehujael begat Methusael. Methusael begat Lamech. He falls asleep in his clothes.

As the week blurs onward, Jesse decides his keepers have been playing careful football with his body clock; they're ringing reveille at cocktail time and calling lunch break after midnight. He could figure the hours, carve hash marks on the walls, but that would violate his compact with the rules. Hell, he's being paid to lie around and daydream and jerk off when he's too bored for anything else. What does Marty say—the secret of enhanced living is to cultivate your hobbies into a career.

Midday on what he suspects is his last, Jesse is sitting at his worktable as a monitor enters with a meal. This one is new, a woman who wears a gray jumpsuit and a sporty, long-billed army cap in the manner of Fidel. Her plentiful burnt-red hair is the only concentrated color he's seen in days. Her ankle socks show lacy eyelets on a scalloped cuff.

"Hey," Jesse says, his voice sandpapery and unfamiliar.

The monitor tries to restrain emotion from her face, but her eyes spark with interest. Jesse gestures at his food.

"There are only six Tater Tots here. I had eight last time. Eight yesterday, eight the day before. You think I'm not paying attention?"

She writes in a small notebook and watches him, her arms clasped in the casual posture of someone looking into a shop window. Jesse spreads his palms in surrender. "Pardon me, silence is golden, it slipped my mind. Just venturing a point, you know, in the interest of science."

The monitor wags a chiding finger; her hair rustles at her shoulders. Henna, coppery as a penny and so freshly applied its scent muds the air long after she's gone.

The afternoon's exam is on an especially relentless section of the Book of Ezra. Jesse's keepers have gotten sloppy and the questions are marred by misspellings and references to material he's sure he hasn't seen. He double-checks his answers, dredges up a lineage of Levite priests and sons of priests in the time of the Babylonian exile. Let the bastards bounce him how they want—this test may be his grand finale, he's going to ace it.

There's a scrabbling in the hallway and the unmistakable clamor of Marty in full throat: "Delta Dawn, what's that flower you have on, could it be a faded rose from days gone by?" As Jesse stumbles to his feet, the door flips open. Marty balances an oily pizza box on his upthrust palm. In the month since Jesse's seen him last, he's regrown his brushy, gray-flecked beard.

"Hey there, lab rat. Miss me?" He swings the door closed with the sharp tip of his boot.

Heat shakes through Jesse's chest. "You're not supposed to be here. How'd you find me?"

Marty drops the pizza on the table and commences measuring heel to toe the yardage between the walls. "Don't let the pie go cold. It's a Hawaiian Special—pineapple and Canadian bacon. Sacrilege, I guess, but who's counting?"

"You're screwing with the data. I'm supposed to be in isolation."

Marty licks his finger to browse the pages of Jesse's exam booklet. "Maybe I *am* the data."

"Which means?"

"Well, there's always layers upon layers, aren't there, the thing observing alters the thing observed. I know a chunk or two about this kind of thing. They tell you the exercise is designed to test your mental faculties under isolation, blah blah blah. Layer one. Who says that's what their hard-on's really for? Maybe they want to push some different buttons, see how you pop or if you pop or when. Maybe they turn warm and loosey-goosey if I drop by to rattle your cage. Hey, for all you know, I'm on the goddamn payroll. Layer two." Marty gives his beard a professorial caress.

"You're serious," Jesse says.

"I take an interest. So, spill it, how've these motherfuckers been yanking your chain?"

Jesse shrugs and tells him how they've fiddled the test questions and the lighting and the time.

"Banzai, Little Brother. I left the Volvo running. We'll hoof it up to Bel's and eat a Hawaiian Special and tell our fortunes."

Jesse summons the energy required to stay in place. "I want to finish what I started."

"Don't put me on," Marty says. "You're being done to, don't you care?"

"It doesn't matter. I made a promise. I want to see how this turns out."

Before he leaves, Marty begrudges Jesse a slim bow. "I guess you'll wear them out long before they dent your stubborn carcass. Kudos."

Jesse sits to review his last five questions. Marty's foxtrot wanes down the corridor, and further along a furnace ignites with an explosive whomp like a boxing glove landing on a bag. The pizza, by some blessing, is furiously hot. Salt and greasy-sweet and sour all at once.

Early next morning a monitor arrives at Jesse's cell with a check for $85. It's the undergrad who signed him in, and he wavers gray-faced at the threshold while Jesse puts on his clothes, the guy rocking back and forth on his Earth Shoes as though in doubt of their ability to hold him up. He has a speech prepared, Jesse realizes, and he waits patiently as the monitor shares thanks for Jesse's invaluable service to the experimental team. His sentences are well-turned and complete; he must have learned the words by rote.

"Don't thank me," Jesse says. "I should be thanking you. It was a gas." He snares the pay envelope from the freshman's fingers. "How'd I tote up? What was my final score?"

"I'm not allowed to say."

"No, sure, that would be telling," Jesse says. He swings onto the corridor, stretching into long, beautiful strides. "Don't ignore my pizza," he calls over his shoulder. "The box is on the floor. You'll want to grade me down for dining off the menu."

Out of doors, Jesse jogs the campus lanes in the general flow toward town. The sunrise seems slicked out of a magazine page, washed hot with the tones of racing-car bodies and cake frostings. Everything feels over-amped: the heavy fragrance of the eucalyptus trees, the cries of the shorebirds that swoop the campus dumpsters. Even the dew cuts a pleasing acid sheen upon his skin. Unbuttoning his coat, he puts on speed down the long curve out of campus, charging through fallen arbor vitae leaves and live-oak scrub on New Year's Day.

Beyond the Glen Coolidge gate he follows a mint-blue VW Bug, which scrapes along the curb at low speed. Out the passenger window a leash runs to the collar of a bounding dog. Jesse feels a twitch of elation—what could toast him better into 1974 than a lazy Santa Cruzan driving her Irish setter on its walk? The woman's voice trickles over the engine burble: good boy, that's it, mama's good boy. Southern molasses.

Through the oval of rear windshield there's a flurry of hennaed hair and a female patch of shoulder and gray sleeve. Yesterday's warder, Jesse's sure of it. Layers upon layers, as Marty would say. When the car slows at a crosswalk, he ambles over to tap hello upon the driver-side window.

He never sees the airborne jolt of red until his legs fly from under him and his head thumps embarrassingly on the pavement. The setter's teeth lock onto his pant cuffs and as he tries to squirm away, Jesse finds himself craning up at the VW's bumper sticker. "Live Simply, So Others May Simply Live."

The woman reacts instantly as though familiar with the procedure. Cooing to the animal, she separates dog from man, shredding pant leg in the process, and pats Jesse onto a bus bench. Back in half a shake, she promises, after she takes her puppy where he won't bother anyone. She'll treat Jesse to a New Year's breakfast, if he'll wait. Carl's a sweet piece of business, really, if you get to know him. The Bug speeds down the street, its rear windshield glazed with the dog's furious breath.

There is a knob the size of a bird's egg on the base of his skull and Jesse feels decorated by a mixture of animal drool and carbon monoxide. Down the road, the VW slithers around a corner halfway into the opposing lane. When she returns, he'll have to ask her name. And then he'll see if he can win a smile from her, the one she hid from him yesterday while registering his sins inside her book.

THIRTEEN

HER NAME IS EMILY SAVONNE and for New Year's she wants to fix them Ramos gin fizzes and a pot of black-eyed peas and rice. Hoppin' John, the dish is called, good luck from New Orleans, where she was raised. "We always drink fizzes New Year's Day," she tells Jesse, "but be careful, they have a habit of leaning up on you. You've had a little tumble and might want to play it safe and stop at one."

Her house is on a low rise overlooking the Pacific, and while the beans simmer and Carl snores beneath their feet, Jesse and Emily sit on the porch and drink and watch a band of surfers run the slate-gray surge. The temperature has fallen and thunderheads collect at the horizon, but the surfers won't give up their play. Their whoops shred into fragments in the wind.

"Amazing," Jesse says. "No fear."

Emily looks at him. "It's incredible out there when it's storming. Ever been?"

"You're kidding."

"The stronger the rain, the wilder the trip. Everything flies through your body—the rain, the current underneath, the waves. Puts you in contact with the deepest region of your soul, I swear."

She is wearing a lightweight cotton dress and she squirms her legs underneath herself as though ashamed of the authority of her feeling. Her face is playful and alive to his examination.

"I guess you're right about this drink," Jesse says.

"I am?"

"You see, I have a sudden desire to take a swim. Came out of nowhere." He stands up and stretches for her hand. "Quick, let's go before I change my mind."

There is a swimming beach a quarter-mile beyond the surfers' lane. Emily slips through the break in total confidence, sleek and rosy in her pink leotard. In his rolled-up jeans, Jesse is happy for a spot near shore where he can scrape the bottom with his toes. The water is warm and fresh smelling and Jesse floats amid the whitecaps, watches Emily swim sidestroke laps out in the calm. If there's anything more beautiful than the female body in action, he doesn't know what it is.

And then the storm launches against them. Emily disappears behind a flare of rain and spray. Jesse calls her name, braces to dive beneath the breakers, searching for a pink blur within the swirling blue. A wave knocks them against each other, his arm somehow cradling around her waist, although the last thing she seems to need is help. Even as they're torn through the surf and dumped onto the shore, Emily is laughing. She's on her feet at once and prods him with a toe.

"Happy New Year, Subject Blue," he hears her say. "You among the living?"

Jesse clambers to his knees. "That was something," he says at last. He can't stop shivering, skin tight with cold.

"Sure was. You good for seconds?"

He hobbles upright, his jeans flapping against his shins. Sand scatters as he hops over broken mussel shells and driftwood shards looking for a smooth spot to set his feet.

"Again...in the water?"

"Sure."

"It's kind of intense out there, don't you think?"

"Certainly is," she says. "I told you, that's why I like it." She sets his hand on her neck just beneath her jaw. "Feel me going?"

Her pulse trips against his fingers, a point of heat almost, a beating spot of light. She's drenched, hair rippled to her skin, yet Emily's manner is so offhand she might be asking him to stroll around the corner. He follows her to the tide line and they wade to their knees through broken kelp and froth. "Whole idea is not to think too much," Emily shouts above the wind.

Jesse stares beyond her—are those lightning traces in the far-off sky? "I knew there was a trick to it," he says. She plunges into the water. He takes a breath and chases behind.

Jesse never saw the couple he and Emily put out there, crown of her head bumping his breastbone, for fuck's sake, and his hands always on her, thinking she'd crackle off in a puff of smoke, if he neglected to ground her. She dug it, nestled close, red hair waggling and that lunatic dog. You wanted to herd them under your wing and shade them from harm.

They were young, remember, nineteen or twenty, and true love, mercy, it's a gooey ball, isn't it, a mess of hope and fear and physical charge. It poured off of them like radio transmission: the lure of every valve cracked wide, all options clear, a fair, broad road. I might have warned Jesse. Loosen up, bro, don't be so certain where you're heading. I bit my tongue. Love, from what I've learned, wiggles away from you the more you hold onto it, but who was I to put them right?

We would hear them stomping downstairs those gloomy February weekends. Late in the day and the crust of sleep or worse on their cheeks, their buttons half-done, their folksy effluence of patchouli and candle grease and many orders of funk. We were amused, the Escalona bunch, tickled by their intentions swinging ahead seasons and years, their glandular optimism. It was a kind of sweetness, really.

We reconvened our Friday drives along Highway 1, a foursome now, with Carl nosing his shaggy muzzle to the breeze. I had a new ride, a Grand Prix bartered from a chop-shop in the Castro. A 1962 convertible, candy-apple red and taken, they claimed, from the Oakland P.D. repo lot. I ran it open to the sky and engine screaming. What's the point of buying American if you don't push things over the edge?

We'd switch license plates for odd or even according to whose day it was for gas. Then fill the tank and blast the radio onto the hearings from D.C. We'd take the curve out of the hairpins while White House flunkies gave sworn testimony. Happiness was our lot, I have to say, we were counterbalanced—two by two. The air resounded with the husky voices of Ivy Leaguers facing stir.

Late in the evening, we'd return to town and commandeer the Escalona living room, roust Paul from bed to be our deejay. Why sleep when we could dance and talk art and insurrection and slump now and again into a murky corner for a squeeze or screw? We'd rally friends from every precinct: U.C. politicos and biker dykes and an ingathering of granola-heads and street people and drugged-out seekers of the dharma. One night in April, the story goes, a reconstructed Miss Patty Hearst—lately in hiding as the revolutionary cadre Tania—chain-drank Mai Tais in our kitchen while laying down the law on Engels and Marcuse. Rumor reports she had a nimble hand upon the blender.

FOURTEEN

ONE SATURDAY IN MARCH, Jesse makes gumbo in Emily's kitchen while she's off at her weekend job. He's never cooked gumbo before, and the recipe's a challenge. He counts twenty-four different ingredients and multiple directions, all of it scrawled on index cards that line up on the counter. He stirs the pot until the roux is dark as peanut butter then adds the rest of the ingredients, jumping back when the pot spits back oil and minced vegetables. He finishes with enough white, black, and red pepper to raise the dead. It's her aunt's recipe, shipped west with Emily when she moved to California.

It's a long stall until his girlfriend comes home, but Jesse loves waiting in her house among her stuff. It's a catalog of everything Emily holds dear—furniture, pictures, clothing, dog. Him. He tastes the soup three times to convince himself he's got it right.

At lunchtime Jesse takes Carl to the beach and eats a leftover burrito while the dog sniffs around. He's still a little wary of the setter, but thank God, dog and man have made a somewhat, semi-steady, kind of peace. Or so Jesse hopes, trying not to show his nerves in front of the animal. The dog canters down the strand, ears flowing, muzzle snapping at the waves. To Jesse's relief, he trots back on call and they troop up the stairs and back home.

Dinnertime is still hours away, so Jesse puts on a record and cleans the kitchen. The floor and counters look like a crime scene, but he gets it done, then moves on to the living room. Pushing a vacuum cleaner around the floors, he's careful not to bump against the Meissen figurines on the side table: a shepherd and his lass that were her mom's. A quick way to see Emily lose it is to break one of her things, a twist in her behavior Jesse's still getting used to. Still, their sometimes fights only add balance to the day. Like negative space in a painting, light and dark working together to make a whole.

After dinner, they walk to town for ice cream. She has a finger curled through one of his belt loops. Jesse slows his pace so Emily can keep up beside him. He could do this for miles and years.

Jesse's birthday comes on the last day in July. Isabel and Emily have planned a daylong visit to Big Sur. It's a Wednesday and the women use the Escalona telephone to call in sick to their employers. Dressed in sarongs and brightly colored leis, they dance a lurid hula around Jesse while he's on the phone with Little Mitch. He mugs alongside them, fancies up his phone conversation with a sickly stammer and an assortment of gargles and groans.

The party continues at the dining table with breakfast mimosas and beignets and sugary birthday kisses from the ladies. Marty demurs. He's beached himself belly upward on the couch after an all-night haul from L.A. A firm of Valley orthodontists is looking to fund his current project— Trouble Bubble Gum, replete with trading cards of the

Watergate witnesses and prosecutors and a comic strip of Nixon done over as an eye-patched Bazooka Joe.

"My medics, you gotta love 'em," Marty calls out to no one in particular. "They got mister-macho sideburns and backyard tennis courts and wives who bop around in walnut-paneled Country Squires. Right-thinking sons of the republic, and in their heart of hearts, you know they feel exposed. They want tax shelters and offshore disbursements. They want refuge from the hungry reach of Uncle Sam. And from how they clocked the cuties sipping Galliano at the Café Fig last night, they want a little laissez faire. Abide with me, I tell them, I'll show you the light *and* the way—plus eighteen points on every buck from dollar one, hundred percent off the books."

Jesse spies the silver tips of Marty's boots flashing a fervent jiggle over the sofa's padded arm. Cocaine, sly son-of-a-bitch, direct from an orthodontist's drug locker. "You've gone to school on them, your new best friends," Jesse says. "I bet you know them better than they know themselves."

Marty stomps to his customary seat at the head of the table. "I follow the old tried and true. Information is money and I want the keys to the bank."

"I don't see where you'll find a nickel in that business," Isabel says. "Nixon's done for, and then who'll care?"

"Tricky's like plutonium, his half-life is forever," Marty says. "Gone from office, we'll sell to the nostalgia crowd." He swipes a beignet from Jesse's plate. "You make your birthday wish?"

Isabel steadies her palm against Marty's thigh. "That's for lunchtime, honey, with the cake."

"Oh, come on," says Marty. "What is this, the Army? Drill at 0-1200?"

"We've been on this all week," Emily says. "All planned the way we like. When you were with your dentists out of town." An angry blush colors her neck and cheeks. Luminous, Jesse judges, lit by the velocity of what she's feeling. He sits back and lets the bubbles in his glass tease his throat. Everything, anger included, can be shaped into the celebration.

Marty produces a weary smile for the entire table. "Hell, don't we want to try some wishes now?" he says. "Wishes now, wishes later—let's pile them on, why be mingy?"

Emily faces Isabel who shrugs in mock despair. "OK, but not out loud," Emily says. "They won't come true."

"Beautiful," Marty says. "The realm of serious attention. Silent only." He presses his fingers to his lips as though in prayer.

It's decided they'll hold hands and Jesse stretches out to Emily and Isabel on either side. As if by command, his friends lower their eyes and calm their breathing—calling up their wishes for him, he can't imagine what. In the fairy stories he loved as a boy, wishes were granted with spite and mined with deadly traps and snares. Only the clever prevailed to see their fantasies come true. Jesse closes his eyes, smelling champagne froth and frangipani and female sweat. At eight or nine, he'd tear through the pages until the ending brought relief. The valedictory always the same: happily ever after.

I was flayed that morning, with intricate nasal chemistry and grit caking my pupils from post-party rebound and fatigue. My mood was less than airy, I admit. Should have given regrets, cashed in on the couch. But I bore down and did my honors as a friend. Christ, twenty-one. You want to make witness, don't you, see your pal through. Besides, the ladies had cooked a Provençal picnic of tapenade and pissaladière. The cake was out of M.F.K. Fisher, whole wheat flour and fresh lavender and brown sugar glaze. How could I pass by my chunk of that?

The women led us on a hike in the Ventana Highlands, a scrubby trail above Big Sur. Bel carried a small machete, took us through manzanita groves and fire-charred undergrowth that smelled of creosote. It seemed to me she pushed us through the meanest route there was. She grunted every time her blade hit wood.

Emily wore flip-flops, a bikini top and sarong, and tore full-speed uphill despite the heat. Brought her back to summers in the Garden District, she told us, excepting this was dry and hardly merited a fuss. She gave us stories of her girlhood, nuns and pralines and gigging frogs with Cousin Luther, sneaking Sazeracs at Galatoire's before she made eighteen. She never once let free of Jesse's hand. I slipped well out of earshot in the rear.

Carl, I can't say why, chuffed round my ankles as though I was his god. I'd never shown him much more than my boot, and his lousy judgment made me sad, so much wasted loyalty and affection. He dragged me on his leash two miles of trail, slobbered my fingers when I stumbled or fell. Let's not build too much on it, OK?—they crave the salt.

While the others set up lunch around a picnic blanket, I climbed atop the tallest boulder on the bluff. The cliff sheared hundreds of feet to the ocean and there were dozens of rocks as black as cancer grinding through the surf—an ugly death for anyone inspired to take an extra step. The sunlight, Jesus, it sledged off the waves and landed on the brain with force. The natural violence California manufactures without thinking.

Forgive me, I had a mighty whiz over the side, one of those luscious streams stretches on for minutes, hours, days. Did wonders, pinked me up body and soul. Standing cock in hand in the out-of-doors binds you with the ages, a cell-memory, I'm thinking, of life in the cave.

"Enjoying the scenery to its fullest?" Isabel had slipped behind my back while I was still exposed. The others and the dog were a few steps farther along.

"You might dig it too if you had the appropriate machinery," I called over my shoulder. I added a small waggle to underline my point.

Isabel appeared only modestly impressed. "I know how to pee outside. I was a Girl Scout once upon a time. I just don't consider it an art form." I plinked a finale and tucked and zipped, stepped down from my perch. "Everything can be art, baby, if you put your mind to it."

Jesse interrupted for toasts and poured out Dixie Cups of Côtes du Ventoux. Emily had tied pigtails in his hair and threaded colored ribbons through the strands. He had the peppy look of a show pony. "Here's to journeys," he said most earnestly.

"Journeys," Isabel and Emily chimed in. Everyone was waiting for me, even Carl gazed fondly upward.

"Happy birthday, partner," I said. "Great days coming." Touched glasses with my friend, had me a slug of fruity red. "Now—where the fuck do you intend that we should go?"

Once voiced, a worthy idea is like a bully, won't let you squirm loose until you submit. There was a debate, of course, a puny struggle over jobs and obligations, but by cake-and-candle time—amazing, by the way, with a fine crumb and mossy as a field in June—we'd booked ourselves a trip to New Orleans by car. That was Jesse's contribution, New Orleans for Sazeracs. He was pleased with himself, stood grinning at the Pacific, his ribbons frisking in the wind.

I lay my head on Carl's dozing flank, watched the clouds shred into tiny pieces. The women rested in the shade of a stunted tamarack and their quiet talking spun on the breeze. How right and good to see my boy take charge. Twenty-one. The world of men.

They come upon the Mississippi in the hot, wet moon-light, looping a roundabout course along the city's edge to view the tanker lights upon the water and to smell the famous mud. Leaning over the convertible's back seat, Marty sprinkles soda pop onto the levee, baptizes their arrival in the true blood of the South. Ever since they crossed the Texas border he's limited his diet to Dr Pepper and Moon Pies and Goo Goo Clusters. To understand the land of Dixie, he declares, you want to be half-whacked on sucrose.

The Savonne house is ringed by wrought-iron fencing, the rails in the shape of corn stalks intertwined with morning glories. Isabel is instantly charmed and gathers everyone to have a closer look. There, in the black metal, she tells them, you can see the maker's stubborn hand—life so irrefutable it's wiggling. "Goddamn gate still has a lock," Marty says as he cuts across the lawn toward the house. "And spikes."

Dewey Savonne is waiting out on the gallery. He's a big man, still in a suit despite the late hour and the weather, and he scoops his daughter off her feet to squeeze her hello. Jesse recognizes the hearty stance from the movies, the posture of someone used to running orders down the line. Mr. Savonne has a shipping business at the Stuyvesant docks. He settles his daughter on the floor stoutly, the way his men must dump their sacks of grain.

"You're the boyfriend, I believe," he says to Jesse. "She told me you were a tall one." He lobs a glance at Jesse's ponytail and puka-shell necklace, the silver stud in his left ear. "Wish I knew why you boys want that girly look. I'm as tolerant as the next man, but help me, didn't your people raise you to dress more carefully than that?"

Emily slaps her daddy on the arm. "Be good. You promised."

"So I did. Sorry, son, I've got a mouth on me. You're welcome to ignore me as often as you like. It's a pleasure to have you and your friends to visit."

"Pleasure's mine," Jesse answers and Dewey pounds a bruising welcome on his back. Physical surplus will be the order of the day in New Orleans. The man's face is swollen with fatherly good cheer.

Unaccountably, Marty is on best behavior and shakes hands as wholeheartedly as a Rotarian. He shadows Dewey into the living room, asking for a cold drink and following his host into the kitchen. Without waiting for an invitation, Isabel explores the downstairs rooms.

"That wasn't halfway bad," Emily says. "Daddy likes you."

From the kitchen comes the rumble of Marty and Dewey's laughter. "If you say so," Jesse says.

Over the living room mantel hangs a silkscreened portrait, Emily's mother, the resemblance undeniable. She's dark and lissome like her daughter and done up in a beaded hat and pearls. The face seems fearless, with lurid shadow lines in fuchsia and green. "Andy Warhol did it from a photograph," Emily tells him. "In '67 most of her friends were ordering up Warhols and Mommy decided she would too, wig and everything. She didn't care how treatment had ruined her or what the painting cost. Twenty thousand dollars, and since the funeral I don't think Daddy's looked at it except sideways once or twice."

His girlfriend is flushed and wet-eyed as though memory has notched her up a few degrees, but no, she slides against him, curves her tongue into his ear. "This sultry weather's got me thinking. I've got a bed upstairs that's never had a boy in it," she says. "And a cheerleader's outfit from St. Sulpice Academy that still might fit. You should catch me with my spangles and pompoms."

"Isn't it rude to jump the daughter of the house without so much as a goodnight to your dad?"

Emily looks to the kitchen and smiles indulgently. "No, the others won't miss us; they'll be swapping lies till past dawn. Now move on upstairs and report for business."

Jesse undresses in the bedroom while Emily ducks into the bathroom to put on her cheerleader's tunic and skirt. Her bed is canopied and made up with lace-bordered linens appliquéd in corn and flowers, the Savonne crest, it seems. The sheets have a rich, loamy smell—of cedar, Jesse decides, picturing a dovetailed chest, hand-carved and in the family for generations. He lies back on the soft percale, swamped in heat, his calves clenched as though he's still in motion. As though he's speeding in the Grand Prix, tires bucking on the pavement and the Gulf air scorching diesel on his face.

For most of a week, Jesse and his friends sweat through the Quarter's historic sites and oyster bars and three or so after-hours clubs each night. There's a rabid quality to Marty's vacation ethic; they're hardly comfortable in one locale before he packs them off to where he wants them next. "We'll rest when we get back to California," he says if anyone pleads for a quieter pace. "Think like sharks, people, like wolves. The only thing that signifies is forward ho."

One afternoon, Jesse and Emily leave Marty and Isobel in the Quarter and peel off by themselves. She shows him the shops on Magazine Street, walks him through Audubon Park, takes him to the high school football field where she had her first kiss. Then they hop the Charles Street trolley downtown to the church where her family worshiped, a hundred-twenty-five-year-old cathedral that looks more like a Disney princess palace than a church. The interior reminds Jesse of an ormolu vase he once saw at the MFA, its surfaces of gilt and cream and decoration.

"I like the smell," he tells her as they walk past incense censers toward the center aisle leading to the altar. "I feel like I just walked into a party." Light pours in through stained glass, turning the world into a confection.

"It's not how it was when I was little," she says. "This place would sometimes lift me up and sometimes scare me silly. The day I celebrated First Communion we had to kiss Archbishop Hannan's ring. Eighty little girls and boys in line, the girls all dressed as brides. Alphabetical, so I was just nearly to the end. The ring was dripping wet with slobber. I ducked my head and faked it. I was petrified of being caught."

Emily's wearing a pale white knee-length dress she found in her closet, a calmer, sweeter version of herself than Jesse's ever seen. He can picture the eleven-year-old she was, among the faithful.

"But you believed?"

"For years, I had nightmares about that ring. My very first sin. But I believed, I did. My hero was the Virgin Mary."

"And then?"

She points him to the vaulted ceiling, then to the filigreed stained-glass windows. "Can't say when, but a day came when it seemed like a great big fairy story. It was just me and Daddy, then. He understood."

"Don't you miss it? No more rings to kiss. No more Virgin Mary. No more certain path to heaven."

She shoots him a darkening look. "We have to grow up, don't we? Live in the world as it is."

Jesse has the sense he's angered her, though he doesn't know how. He thinks they should go find Marty and Isabel. "I want some sunlight on my face and a drink in my belly," he tells her and she nods OK. She leads him through the Quarter looking for their friends.

At breakfast near the end of the visit, Emily's father invites Jesse to a round of golf at the Audubon Club. It's Dewey's opinion that nothing would bless the day better than playing hooky from the office. The two of them can get to know each other better, enjoy the feel of grass beneath their shoes.

"And after we pass by the club, we'll go on over to the Fair Grounds and I'll buy us a po' boy at the clubhouse, we'll watch the fillies run." Mr. Savonne stands by the table, rubs his large pink hands together at the pleasurable notion. "Tee-off's in half an hour, son, give you a chance to make yourself pretty before we go."

Jesse looks at Marty who sips his coffee and gazes back placidly.

"Don't be bashful," Dewey says to Jesse. "If you've got something to say, I'm listening."

"The four of us have arrangements to drive out to Tant' Adele's, Daddy," Emily says.

"We were going to take a boat out on the water," Jesse says. "Emily promised us some alligator pie."

"Don't let me slow you down," Dewey says, in a show of Southern graciousness. "Adele's alligator's worth the drive. You folks have your day."

"What kind of course is Audubon?" Marty wants to know. "Does it run long or short?"

"Short and snaky," Dewey answers. "The greens are fast. They'll humble you if you don't know what you're up to."

"A course that informs you who you are," Marty says. "Golf's a great teacher."

Isabel raises her eyes from the leather-bound Baudelaire she shagged from the household library in one of her nightly prowls. "I don't want to miss the bayous, Marty."

He tightens his mouth as though figuring an equation. "Right, babe," he says. "Whatever the good lady says."

It seems to Jesse, Dewey's impossibly delighted that his offer's gone awry. He's whistling as he buckles his briefcase, checks his pocket for his Racing Form and cigars.

"If it's OK with you, I changed my mind," Jesse says. "Let's go to Audubon and the track. Sounds great."

"You're sure? I'm a faithful milk horse, son. I trot to the office without looking."

No, Jesse insists, he wants to go. It will be interesting and fun.

Dewey's Fleetwood is new and white and waxed so recently Jesse can smell carnauba as he opens the door. As they drive away, Emily's father cradles his arm across Jesse's shoulder for a paternal squeeze, then he puts his mouth around an unlit panatela.

"You a betting man?"

"Not especially," says Jesse.

"We'll have to do something about that," Dewey says and he spits out the window.

FIFTEEN

DEWEY AND JESSE'S LOCKER ROOM COMPANIONS are suntanned fellows in their fifties and sixties whose fashion sense runs to sherbet-colored double-knits and mismatched plaids. Zipping into their golfing clothes, they wolf down morning eye-openers while roaring at the punch lines of their dirty jokes. Jesse arranges himself before a floor-to-ceiling mirror. His canary leisure suit—courtesy of Dewey and the Audubon Club pro shop—broadcasts a chemical sheen. Fabric brought to market by the happy folks who manufacture napalm and Twinkies. He salutes his new image, planting his rented golf shoes into the damp wall-to-wall. Ten more minutes, he'll be voting Republican.

Dewey lounges on a locker bench in the company of his pals, amid hairy backs and beer bellies and more unclipped foreskins than Jesse's ever seen. Savonne introduces Jesse as Emily's honeybunch, and the other men take it up like a new hobby, baiting Jesse at each break in the conversation: "Hey, honeybunch, we're bored and ignorant. You know any stories you can throw our way? Jew jokes, Irish, Negro, we're not fancy." "Show us your draft card, won't you, honeybunch? Say boo, we'll walk you on over by Magazine Street to the recruiting officer. Ship you to Nam swift as grease through a goose—Navy, Marines, even Airborne, you got the stuff for the 101st."

Jesse masks his face in innocence and lets the banter wash him by. Marty would know how to meet these guys head-on and charm them into co-conspirators. Without his silver touch, silence and bashful retreat will have to do. Finally, Jesse and Dewey emerge into the sunlight and approach the first tee. Emily's father addresses his ball without preliminaries: one corkscrew of his hips and the ball flies up and out with a sound like a pistol shot. Jesse's hands are shaking as he balances his Titleist on its tee.

Dewey moves behind him without being asked, molds Jesse's elbows and legs into proper array. "Careful piece of business, how you managed yourself in the locker room," Savonne says, stepping back to observe his handiwork. "Going along to get along, that's how the wide world likes it. Golf's about the same. The secret is, allow the body to run the deal. Pin your elbows in, turn your mind off, and show the old man what you got."

Crows flock beneath a nearby pepper tree, squawking and fighting over something on the ground. Jesse lets the noise take him over and the coppery scent of the foliage, then slams his wood against the ball. A spray of sod and dirt, a glare of white too white to mark against the sun. Somehow, fortune shining down, his shot goes a respectable distance along the fairway. In silent pleasure, the two men tote their bags to their next position.

Dewey stalks the front nine without a letup, and Jesse watches how he makes his game, powering his shots with overkill and unblinking concentration. He mimics Dewey's method as fairly as he can, scarring the bluegrass with divots, tasting his effort as a swill of turf and caught-in breath and sweat. Happily, he delivers an acceptable drive or putt every few holes. By midday his joints are oiled, his palms blistered, his brain sun-smacked into cheery stupefaction. Jesse's losing, naturally, buck-fifty a stroke, down $45 and doomed for more.

"You're putting me in trouble," Dewey tells him. "How'm I going face my little girl if I take all your money? She'll have my skin."

Jesse lines up a putt, strokes, misses. "Is the pressure getting to you?"

Dewey laughs. "Do me a kindness. Try your hardest, will you, son?"

"Can do," Jesse says and misses again.

Into their third hour, Dewey's pace becomes more thoughtful; his swing loses some of its punch. Jesse makes a show of quick-stepping from hole to hole, working up a lather while the older man follows behind. At the fifteenth tee, Jesse straightens his collar and fluffs the creases of his pants. For your victory photo, he explains.

"The game isn't over yet," says Dewey. "Put your mind on success, why don't you?"

"Even when I have no chance?" Jesse asks.

"That's when it's called for," Dewey says.

The next hole is a par four dog-leg that skirts Magazine Street and the course parking lot. As he squares his club head for the tee-shot, Jesse spots the carmine flank of a Grand Prix catty-cornered across two spaces in the rear. He stares at it for a few seconds, listening to the streetcars rattling at the Audubon light. It's Marty's, dripping sunlight and going nowhere. Jesse points his two-iron at the car. "We've got company," he says.

"How's that for something," says Dewey. "Years and years, I've been asking Emily to watch her daddy play—not so much as a maybe. I guess boyfriend ranks a little higher on the tree. You best decide on a shot before we're set upon."

"Sorry," Jesse says. "Too late."

A golf cart steers toward them, Marty squeezed between the two women on a seat made for two. They wave their arms in ragged greeting as though calling for rescue. Jesse takes in his girlfriend's sunburnt, love-struck face, then stoops to check his ball upon its tee. His drive is low and slicking toward the rough, but long. Green in two.

Their day was cursed one side to the other, Emily professes, with a flat tire, a roadside fire ant assault, and a no-neck Yat in a pickup who rode them into the kudzu because he didn't like the ankh sign on their bumper. They never got halfway to Bayou Boeuf. She's wound up, prancing from one bare foot to the other, ready for handsprings. Her toenails are newly painted, a soft coral like the inside of her mouth.

Marty has Dewey by the elbow. "Your little girl was our cool customer, you should have seen her. She got that throwback's license number while I was still checking to see if I had all my parts." His face is raked with scratches. He looks from Dewey to Jesse with the satisfied grin of a man whose day has counted for something. Jesse finds it awkward to be holding his club. He stuffs the iron in its bag.

Isabel slouches against the cart, frowning into the sun. "You're very yellow," she tells Jesse. She plays her fingers over his sleeve. "Like a piece of meringue pie." The scent of Southern Comfort carries toward him. She's drunk and he wonders how much, how long.

"You had yourselves an adventure," he says. "And here I was, trying to hit a little ball into a little hole."

Isabel takes off her sunglasses to stare at him. She seems broody and dulled, as though she's spent a long, gray day bundled up in comforters. "The game of kings," she says. "Are we having a jolly old time?"

"Dewey's chewed me up in little pieces. He's won everything I have in my wallet and half my next week's wages. He likes me, we're simpatico."

Isabel sighs. "Dewey Savonne and the rest of them can't bear losers; they're a blot on the flag." She finishes what's in her flask and cocks her arm and flings the bottle as far as she can throw. "Alley oop," she says and moves toward the others, stumbling nearly to her knees and laughing herself upright. "The heat," she calls out in explanation. "I'm very fine."

Marty has convinced Dewey to let him hit the last four holes, and his natural ability and luck wilts the remainder of Jesse's game into a run of double and triple bogeys. Everyone puts on their best manners. There are St. Sulpice cheers—a surfeit of laughter and rah rah. By the last hole, when he is four over par and still on the green, Jesse's self-mockeries run dry, his spirit lags. Mercifully, Dewey shoos the others to the clubhouse for its famous whiskey punch. As Jesse tips his golf ball into the eighteenth cup, he can see them at a table in the patio. Marty is on his feet, demonstrating his swing.

"You've got stamina, son," Dewey says. "I commend you."

Jesse pulls out his money. "Good, it will get me through the painful part of paying off my debt."

The sun has reddened the tips of Dewey's ears, lent his face a pleasant glow that confounds Isabel's claim of kill or be killed. Savonne waves off Jesse's offer.

"We can pretend you paid. Just don't let on to Emily. As you might have learned, she's a stickler."

On the patio, Emily is up beside Marty, taking a lesson, tossing her red hair into the sunlight as she whips her arms over her shoulders. "She loves you a lot, doesn't she," Jesse asks.

Dewey seems surprised by the question. "Of course she does. Is that so strange?"

Jesse thinks of his parents, his high school Sunday dinners, a long corridor of dry London broil, the pitter-pat of silverware on Melmac plates.

"It's a big world," Jesse suggests.

At the patio entrance, Dewey stops them to kick the dirt out of his spikes and waits for Jesse to do the same. "You're the first young man she's brought around, you know."

Jesse says, "I wouldn't make so much of that."

Dewey nods, runs the horn of his palm over Jesse's back to brush away a spray of dirt and grass. "I wouldn't either if I were you," he says. "I think she's sleeping with your friend."

Jesse hears the words and looks to the patio table. Marty and Emily are caught up in their game but Isabel faces him, a sorrowful and drunken smile trembling on her lips.

Dewey asks, "You going to be all right?"

"Tell them I went home," Jesse says.

SIXTEEN

Nixon resigned that night, his gloomy puss on national TV, every nerve exposed, every twitch on display. His voice rippled with sanctity and paranoia, and we could see that he was tweaked on potent meds. Downers was my guess, goofballs, he looked the type. We sat our dinners on our laps and watched on Dewey's console RCA; we cheered when the man said he was leaving. But a trickle of uncertainty swam in my gut. Nixon's cockroach soul was ballast to our youth, our lack of restraint, the glee we brought to our living. Without him we'd be off compass—who could calculate the effect?

I took my melancholy outside and we walked to the Quarter, Emily and Isabel and I. There was street zydeco and old women hawking andouille po' boys and barbecued shrimp, the whole world dancing the Crescent City Shuffle decked out in Nixon masks. We wandered the edges where the riffraff collected, the drunks, the spare-changers and runaways, flotsam so transported they couldn't talk or hear or think. We handed out sandwiches and quarters, emptied our pockets, and drank Hurricanes from go-cups, stumbling to the music as the night rang down in humid waves. Jesse was gone, making miles on a Greyhound and feeling betrayed. The body does what it must, Little Brother, what it's bred for. Some people can't bear the news, I understand.

The rest of the summer and into fall, the women and I stayed out of Santa Cruz, thinking we'd spare Jesse, let a callus build between us. We moved Emily to the redwoods and spent our hours on Isabel's deck, reading the classics out loud, Melville and Conrad, those bulky sentences filled with philosophical murk. We put food on the grill and ran to bed before we came to table, slammed against each other as though we were cattle or machines. It's a complex geometry, three in bed, and we lived in a state of self-awareness and unrest. We set one rule to keep the peace: no private frolics one on one. Emily laid down the hammer on it, our little colonel. Diligence was required, an organizing principle, or we'd do harm.

We failed, though, didn't we, showered hurt in every quarter before we were through. Love's unruly and unrepentant, a merciless entanglement I barely understood. By late October, Emily and I could not ignore what we were feeling for each other. We grabbed the dog and stashed him with a friend, wrote Isabel a note and fled the country. We learned our tricks from Tricky Dick. Scorch the earth and don't look back. Destruction, like almost everything, is in the mind of the beholder.

Throughout the fall, Jesse demands as much overtime as Whole Earth Retreads can send his way. He trains himself on the extruder, becomes the floor boss of the graveyard shift, watching with fascination as molten tread shapes a new face onto the bludgeoned tires in his pile. When the morning crew comes in, Jesse salves his burns and jogs to campus where he sneaks a place in a life class at U.C. He claims an easel closest to the door, laying charcoal on his page while keeping the corner of his eye on the instructor. The models are all women, wholesome California blondies, and Jesse absorbs himself into setting down his lines and rubbing shadows with his thumb, time fallen away. He struggles to bring alive what it is that makes the women beautiful: their ease, their boredom, how they wear their bodies like a perfect shell.

In the afternoon, he goes to bed and drifts on the border of sleep. When he closes his eyes, he urges the models to mind, their nipples, hipbones—one always smells of spoiled fruit as though she's recently been fucked. He masturbates grimly, in repetition, feeling little but the heat of come against his leg. Downstairs, his roommates make their supper, play music, talk on the phone; there are arguments, the slamming of the screen door, Natalie running her meetings, giving orders to her troops. Jesse can picture her, in her glory, hands on her hips and leading with her stubborn chin. Under his covers, his legs grind restlessly. His clock ticks like a second heart. The alarm is set for eleven o'clock.

One day in late October at close of shift, Isabel is waiting on the sidewalk near the factory loading dock. The morning is overcast and cold and she's bundled into a sweater of home-spun wool. Her bicycle leans against a laurel tree that's planted in the verge of grass at the sidewalk's edge. The foliage casts her in a somber, gray-green light.

Jesse rests his portfolio between them. "This is how it comes down?" he says. "You just show up?"

"I didn't think about it too closely." She touches the burn that scars his wrist. "I don't like you on the midnight shift. It's dangerous."

"You don't have to worry about me," he says. "I get by. I fucking triumph."

She looks at him with her steady gaze, the one she's trained to snip out leather patterns to a feather edge. "You're doing art again? I called the house, they said I might have to search for you on campus."

"I'm not shaking any walls," says Jesse. "It fills my day."

Around them, departing workers descend the loading dock to the street, talking in Spanish and English, a torrent of Portuguese—the Sayao sisters, famous for their tempers and their flan. They stop their squabbling and nod, extend to Jesse the respectful distance due the patrón.

Isabel watches them walk off. "They treat you like the boss."

"What I am. Midnight to eight."

"You're not serious?" Isabel says. "Is that what you want, cracking the whip to speed up the line?"

"What I want," Jesse says with some urgency, "doesn't feature into it."

Isabel hesitates before taking Jesse's hand in both of hers. "No," she says. "I guess it doesn't."

There's a tremor in her fingers and looming sadness on her face as she describes Marty and Emily's flight, how they fell in love and might be getting married.

"And I'd heard it was only roses and sunshine after New Orleans," Jesse says. "Smash couplism, wasn't that your motto? The revolution for real."

"Nothing was real," she says. "Except what we did to you." Her eyes well and what can Jesse do but circle her in his arms? The portfolio catches them at their ankles. He kicks it out of the way.

"Careful," Isabel says. "Your work."

Jesse holds her cautiously—the damp wool and her body rigid beneath, her breath spiky with exhaustion, her few tears. He tells her, "Come to the house, I'll make you something wonderful for breakfast. You can walk me up the hill."

"That's how we got started," she says softly. Trouble has changed her, made her visible at last.

"Different hill," Jesse says. They walk together up the grade in silence.

After breakfast, they decide to have a day of it, tramping miles through the redwood groves above the campus and ending at Lulu's for pork adobo and too much rum. Isabel shifts between tears and apologies and fury; she leaves out nothing, even the specifics of how she and Marty and Emily were in bed.

Jesse listens in a state of dull fatigue, aware of Lulu behind them in her doorway. She's watching them, clicking her fingers to the jukebox beat. "Why don't we leave the past where it belongs?" he says. "Convenient amnesia, I'm a big fan."

"No, I can't be trusted. You have to see me as I am."

"I see you. You're drunk and beautiful and kind of sad—you're you," Jesse says. "And I am way too wiped for work. I need my nap." Isabel fishes an arm through his to make it out the door.

At Escalona House, Isabel climbs the stairs as though by habit. She smooths a place on Jesse's bed, sits and undoes her braid, staring out the window at the thickening fog. Jesse watches at the threshold. Her hands are cracked and cut and stained with leather dye; they show her age. But they perform with animal deftness, finding an easy way in the dark. She turns to Jesse, puts a finger to her lips as he tries to speak. She slips out of her sweater and reaches up with a tiny sigh of desire or regret. "They went to Irian Jaya," she says, murmuring into his neck. "I don't even know where that is."

SEVENTEEN

ISABEL SLEEPS WITH HER LEGS AND ARMS CROWDING the full width of the mattress. Don't let me be a bully, she's said to Jesse—bop me once or twice and I'll roll over. But if he tries even a flimsy tap, she rouses herself in a snarl of dislocation, as though her dreams were filled with violence and pain. Slowly, her eyes pool into focus and she pastes herself against him, her nightgown swimming toward her throat. They make love in a daze, bruising each other in the dark.

Back on eight to four in the truck tire bay, Jesse's lost the approval of his bosses, and he's given up his raise. He's drifted low in the sight of his old partner, Henry Johnson. Jesse's a fool, Henry says, to turn down cash in favor of a little bit of squeeze, no matter how fine.

"You love her, boy?" Henry calls to him one morning as they unload a trailer. Jesse stiffens his back.

"We don't talk like that. We live in the now."

The rain's been falling steadily since dawn. It lays a clatter over the rumble of the idling trucks.

"Live in the now, maybe the lady does," says Henry. "She's got you fussing on her as she pleases. But love's all over you, boy. I can smell it a mile off. In love with yourself, too, appreciating what you think love's done to you. That's even worse."

Jesse dumps a box of tread onto the floor, and a pall of dust spills over the toes of his work boots. "You know a lot about the subject."

"I've got thirty years of track under me, should be enough to recognize upside down from right side up. You're sailing now, think you've got it made, pussy every night, hot coffee in the morning. You wait—one day she'll try and drop some changes over you, tell you how to dress or spend your money, what kind of car to drive. Do as she says, she'll hate you for being her monkey. Don't, and it's nothing but fighting the whole day through. Of course you're right to hang in there while the loving's good."

"Thank you very much, Dear Abby," Jesse says. "Look, we're not in love, we're friends. We care for each other. A human feeling. That's not going to change, whatever goes down."

Henry nods his head and smiles his sharp smile. "You got it figured, then," he says.

"You bet I do," says Jesse. He'll take her to Lulu's tonight and move her around the floor. They're good together when they're dancing.

You've got to love Jesse's hopeful thinking, the trajectory of his belief. There he was, playing in the bigs, making it up as he went along and doing almost all right. He was working toward a goal he didn't even know he had—to turn himself into the kind of man that Isabel would be happy with forever. I can figure how he ran it, that he could estimate her moods, chart a tangent, keep to the shallows. It's more than I could do, but still, I wish he'd toughed it out;

life would have been better for us all. A for effort, pal, high points for hanging in the game.

Bel was turned inward those days, especially on Sunday nights. I'd seen my fill of them, the lady rolling roaches into joints at her kitchen table, dipping them in Mexican vanilla to bring some honey to the smoke. Her freezing kitchen, rain hounding the windows and walls, Isabel cuddled up in deer-skin gloves and booties, her robe buttoned to her neck. She'd be getting high by her lonesome, walled into a gloom so dark and concentrated the drug could barely chip its surface. Jesse'd have to stay away from her, no gentle word or there'd be havoc.

They'd be sore and rattled from over-fucking, the day diluted in bed, looking toward quantity where quality had fallen away. They never said "I love you" to each other. That's a pity, isn't it? Why couldn't Jesse have pushed himself to have his say one of those bitter Sunday nights? Why didn't he barge in and disturb the peace? It might have made a difference in the end. Isabel couldn't have heard it very often, maybe never. Never from me, sweet on her as I was. "I love you" would have whacked some life into that kitchen, upped the kilo-watts so high you could have smelled the heat. He might have won her, changed our story forever. Christ, win her or not, he could have had the worth of claiming everything he felt.

Jesse waits by the tub while Isabel takes a bath. Her eyes are closed and her face is glossy with contentment. This is how he loves to think of her, slumped and undefended. He passes his hand through the water and Isabel's eyes spark awake, then stall. She's considerably stoned—it's possible she isn't sure he's really there.

"I didn't know you'd come in," she says.

"I should paint you like this. Next time I'll bring in my easel."

Isabel shakes her head in mild dismay and stands for Jesse to towel her off, silent as he dries her hair and hands and feet. In the muscle of her left calf, just above the ankle, there's a faded scar. An old tattoo with the ink burnt away, a miniature thunderbolt with feathered wings. It's a relic of ten years ago or more, he's never felt comfortable to ask. Jesse lays his fingertips over the mark as though it were Braille.

"Don't," says Isabel. "I want you up here."

"I never would've let you take it off."

Isabel rests her palms on the top of his head. "I forget how young you are. A baby."

When Jesse stands up, Isabel is fighting tears. She turns away from him and walks herself to bed. Jesse kneels again to pull the bathtub stopper. The water spirals down the drain.

At first light, Isabel's in the living room behind her Singer, her foot laying on the treadle as though she's running laps. She's embroidering onto the yoke of a leather vest, intricate stitches that flesh out the body of a green and yellow snake. Jesse brings her some tea.

"The snake looks like it could bite," he says. "If I were you, I'd dump Rags to Riches and think about a shop of your own. You could put me at the counter."

Isabel hugs her arms around herself, taking consolation from the touch of her body.

"There's no stopping you, is there?" she says. "Your bottomless good nature?"

"I was only trying to be encouraging."

"No you weren't. I feel it even when you're not here. You'd be happy if you could live inside my head."

"That's not what I want."

She stares at him and returns to her stitching.

"I was living in Laurel Canyon when I got the thunderbolt on my ankle. The man I was with decided we were going to TJ to get matching ones. Twins in the skin, was how he put it. I was married to him for three years. Jimmy Lantana, he taught me how to hotwire a car and that's about the whole story."

"You don't have to do this," Jesse says.

"No, I want to, now." Isabel's voice becomes distilled and matter-of-fact. Her mother had a fondness for Metrecal, vodka stingers and *Beat the Clock*; her dad managed the order desk at Pep Boys before he keeled over at a bowling alley when Isabel was twelve. She met Jimmy Lantana in high school and followed him to the Hollywood Hills after they graduated in '64. Isabel worked the lunch shift at Musso and Frank while Jimmy surfed.

"I had an amazing pair of boots, pony leather with the most beautiful fringe way over my calves, and Jimmy and I danced almost every night at the Whiskey. We had a scene there, a kind of vagabond family where everybody was on the verge of glory—musicians and dancers and what have you. I found a weekend job sewing costumes for the bands, groups nobody remembers anymore, for good reason. But one night Jimmy hit me and nearly broke my jaw. I wouldn't get on my knees for a disc jockey who promised to set me up with the costumer for Gary Lewis & the Playboys. Jimmy hit me and then he burst out crying, can you believe it? I couldn't cry, not a single blessed teardrop. I closed the door behind me and never went back, abandoned everything I owned. I think about those boots sometimes."

The sewing machine stops, and Isabel looks at Jesse. The sunlight underlines the weariness on her face. "There it is, or almost. Enough anyway of what you were waiting for, the portrait you wish you could paint. So I want you to go, now, Jesse, go home to your friends on Escalona Court. It was mean of me to get involved with you, selfishness or spite. Revenge on Marty. We're stopping it this morning."

"Wait," says Jesse. "What are you talking about? Back up here."

"Don't be difficult, please don't, you have no ability for it. I want to do this before I learn to hate you. Before you hate me."

He makes an effort to go to her, but her posture holds him at bay—her tight grip on the edge of the sewing table as though she might sink from sight.

"Let's have breakfast and talk this out," he says. "We could go for a walk—no questions, no days of old, just the tall trees and our feet in the mud and whatever you need to say."

Isabel shakes her head. "No."

"We're breaking up? Out of nowhere, just like that?"

"We were never together," Isabel says. Her voice softens. "You'll thank me later."

She stands in the doorway while he throws his things into a paper bag and walks out her drive to hitchhike home. His last memory of her is a half-wave goodbye, the arm jerked down as soon as he turns for a goodbye wave of his own.

Jesse's housemates are glad to see him and he fills his winter evenings by cooking dinners from Le Cordon Bleu and Julia Child. After supper, he follows Lucy for chanting in the damp backyard. The mantra will cool out the thinking motor, Lucy tells him. Notice but don't judge what wanders through your brain. Impossible, Jesse decides, though he folds his legs into a passable lotus posture and matches his breath to an inner count. He can last ten minutes before leaving Lucy to herself.

Sometimes, at the end of the day, Jesse walks by Rags to Riches. He tests himself, heart stilled, seeing what he can pick out through the display window. There are pieces of movement smeared through the glass, car headlights and customers at the changing mirror, Steely Dan at high volume on the stereo. No scrap of Isabel, though, her well-turned step. The walk home lasts twenty minutes, the wind at his back.

In late December, Jesse flies the redeye to Boston for a holiday visit with his parents. Although his mother has breakfast on the table, Jesse jogs out into the neighborhood the first morning, kicking a trail through the crust of frozen sand and half-melted snow. Almost every house but his is mobbed by multicolored lights and life-size plastic Santas—an assault of seasonal goodwill and low-rent taste. After more than an hour Jesse comes home muddied to the shins and shaking with hunger. His mother watches him eat his pancakes. She piles second helpings on his plate before he asks.

"You're getting healthy out there in California?" she says. "I never knew you as a jogger."

"I jog now, I eat sprouts. Sometimes I do yoga. I haven't had a hotdog in a year."

Louis Kerf has been charting stock prices on an index card. It's an exercise he's done as long as Jesse can remember, investing make-believe money and keeping score. "Leave him be, Barbara," he says. "The boy flew all night. He won't know which end is which."

Jesse licks syrup off his fork. "These are perfect," he tells his mother. "Worth the trip for sure."

His father expects him to put in time at the store and Jesse obliges, dim long hours in the backroom inventorying fasteners and nuts and nails, more varieties and sizes than the mind can absorb. Hours of this and the spirit drains to absolute zero, he'll have to tell Lucy—the hardware way to Zen.

After dinner, Jesse settles into the TV room with his parents, watching Flip Wilson and Dean Martin, a lost empire of Vegas comics and finger-popping belters of the old school. His mother gossips above the programs, catalogs the tribulations of family friends Jesse hasn't thought about for years. Their children, to a soul, are drug-addicted, locked away in loony wards, or vanished into the Haight or Gastown or distant parts unknown.

"Is this a warning or a compliment?" Jesse asks.

"Can't we watch the show without the chitchat?" his father says, pushing up the TV volume with his clicker. "These Gold Digger girls, look how high they kick."

The airport bus dumps Jesse and his luggage in the center of downtown Santa Cruz among the Frisbee players, sidewalk balladeers, and roach clip merchants, everyone brought out by unseasonably warm weather. There is no one he recognizes, but Jesse feels the balmy weightlessness of being among his own. The thin January sun is on his face, and what he wants is to have a look at Isabel.

This time, she's right where he wants her, as though called out by his imagination, sweeping up in the open doorway of her store. Or the back of her, anyway, muscles bunched beneath a T-shirt as she pushes her broom. It should be simple—to say hello—but she moves inside and flings her arms around someone who swoops her up for a midair kiss. His face is hidden by the shadows and by a long fall of gray-streaked curls, but the gesture is indelibly Marty's. Jesse watches them kiss and part, Marty setting Isabel down lightly. Jesse holds back for a minute, deciding what to do. He's tended his anger so carefully, pointing it at one of them or the other, at both together—at himself—he's nearly breathless. And then he looks at Isabel again—the way she folds into Marty's embrace and stays there. When Jesse walks in the shop door, his head is pounding, as if he's surfaced after a too-long ocean dive.

He stands in the doorway, enjoying the surprise crossing their faces. "Hey there," he says. "Long time."

Marty's tender in their reunion—he keeps patting Jesse's shoulder, ruffling his hair. Isabel watches from a distance. She holds onto her broom as if she's forgotten what it's for, a quiver in her lips. But then she melts. It's embraces all around, their troubles leached away by the astonishment of being together and just friends once more. Everybody talks at once, and laughs, and talks some more.

Marty, of course, has hours of stories, and after dinner on Isabel's back deck, Marty slides Emily into the conversation, the slimmest bit of her, as though she were one more scenic postcard from the trip. She's gone back to Louisiana, Marty tells them, made homesick by Asia's heat and ferment. Isabel leans her cheek to Jesse's, mutters something too low for Marty to hear. Forgive me. He doesn't reply at first, soaks in her scent and touch.

Her face brims with pleasure as Marty acts out the proper technique for fishing Burma's Inle Lake, the fisherman standing with his leg crooked over the oar, pulling fish into his net.

We're fine," Jesse tells her. "Always were, always will be."

EIGHTEEN

MARTY CELEBRATES HIS RETURN with a new preoccupation, drumming on the dozen iron gongs he's carted home from Indonesia. No matter the weather, he practices in the Escalona backyard, bare to the waist, his batik trousers fog-damp and pasted to his ankles. His rubber mallets build a wall of discord, and it's amazing, Jesse thinks, Marty's accelerating skill, the pandemonium he produces and the release. All in the style of the gamelan master who tutored him at the foot of Bali's Mount Agung.

"Ten years ago, Agung exploded," Marty explains to Jesse and Isabel after an hour-long impromptu one February night. "First eruption in a century, and hundreds died, thousands, all of them chanting and dancing in a ceremony to one of their gods or demons—they've got millions, Buddhist, Hindu, Moslem, the Balinese are ecumenical like that. Think of it, there they were, in a religious frenzy three yards from heaven when the ash plume hit. Asia cuts it straight to the bone—nothing but eight kinds of crazy crashing in on you from every side there is, and nobody wants it any different."

"That seems horrible and cruel," Isabel says. "What—the universe's just a monster? Nothing but spite and chaos?" She's been solemn tonight, sitting on the lanai, observing Marty at his music with her hands in her lap. "Some of us believe everything happens for a reason, even when we can't see one."

Marty's eyes soften in pity. "What I saw was the cinder trail, six villages nothing but ash and mud and the occasional bone. It's hard to find God's love in that."

"Here's what *I* believe," Jesse says. "I believe we drink some Cuba libres and forget about which one of you is right."

Marty rises behind his array of gongs and comes to them. He's sweaty from his playing—an odor shines off him feral enough to prickle the throat. "Aren't you going to take a stand, lay some money on your own set of convictions?" Marty says to Jesse. "It's balmy there on the sidelines, but Christ, it's boring."

"I'm for wait-and-see until more evidence shows up one way or the other," Jesse says. "I'm looking for my sign."

Marty sighs—slamming the music out of his gongs has run the battle out of him. He lays his head on Isabel's lap and shuts his eyes. Her fingers play with his curls; she has a look of faraway. Rags to Riches went bankrupt yesterday, a day before the two-week payroll was due. Isabel skates by her mortgage payments month to month, nothing to spare.

"Maybe we should put our heads together, think about how to cushion you for now," Jesse tells her.

"I don't want to think. Not for a minute."

"You heard the lady," Marty says. "Thinking's not to the point. Faith will provide. The unseen hand."

"In case it doesn't, I've got $600 I can toss in toward your house payment," Jesse says. "Loan's good as long as you need it."

Isabel slides Marty off her lap. "I want to dance," she says. "Lulu's calls. Don't bother to get up, I'm going by myself." The two men watch her leave.

"I love it," Jesse says. "She might lose her house, but there she goes to shake her stuff. Maybe we should tag along."

"Spare the lady some oxygen, haven't you learned by now? Besides, there are wheels in motion. Give me a few more days, we'll all be in the roses, Bel included. Just don't bug me for details, you might jinx my deal." Leaning a hand against Jesse's shoulder to hoist himself to his feet, Marty walks off to take a shower.

For a little while, Jesse stays out on the lanai. The wind is moving through the trees and Marty's instruments are chiming on their own, a scattering of phantom tones. Jesse approaches the gamelan, touches the carved teak struts, the brass fittings—so much exacting detail—then strikes the largest gong with his fist. The clang is muffled, vibration charging up his arm and into his shoulder. He hits again using a rock this time. The sound booms deep as church bells.

I did my tap dance three days later during dinner with the Escalona crew, how I was grabbing up the lease on Rags to Riches and putting Isabel and Jesse in charge. I was thinking not to sell too hard—modesty only—but my friends were used to the froth, so when the food was steaming on our plates—gado gado and satay that Jesse helped me grill—I popped some T-shirts from beneath the table and waited until everybody put one on. The lettering was fresh from the printer, colors as shiny as the sauces we were wiping off our chins. Isabel had done a logo of a grinning monkey with its tail on fire. Hanuman Designs, I announced—after the Hindu monkey god, the hero of the Upanishads, good luck in all his incarnations.

I rolled out the high points—how my Indonesian contacts had a cornucopia of righteous stuff for us to sell: silver jewelry, carved wood masks, and woven wall hangings, and what would be our central business, exotic leather goods—cobra, lizard, ostrich, frog—my guy in Denpasar'd sew anything that crawled into whatever we wanted. Isabel was designing a line of clothing for the U.S. market. Cheapo headbands and trinkets for the street freaks and teeny-boppers, fancier bags and belts for the moneyed gentry. Jesse would run the import side and shop administration. I'd be Mr. Outside, working our concept and marketing, finding investment, playing to my strengths.

It'd be a blast—how couldn't it—we'd run the store at constant party volume and shovel money in our pockets, even-Steven all around. What we needed from the housemates was some upfront grunt work sanding floors and painting walls. Later, hours here and there at the register or helping Jesse in the backroom filling orders.

I was ready for Lucy and Natalie to turn down their lefty noses at my offer. Money was part of the death culture, after all, and they couldn't let it stain their hands. But I'd made sure to tell some stories of our workers overseas, how cottage industry would nurture independence for the mostly female artisans. Imagine my surprise when Nat and Luce signed on soon as I finished. They made me promise I'd donate to the S.C. women's shelter a percent to be determined of the profits. Right-o, I said. Let our good fortune spread equal karma, the Balinese are more than hip to that, and we can be, too.

Jesse, on the other hand, looked queasy. My eye was on him as he fought what he was feeling, objection written on his face like a rash. Fear of his ability to lead, maybe, so scared of failure he didn't want to start. As the night went on I was hoping he'd cheer up and be bobbed along by the general confidence, get what it meant I wanted him in charge. But he moped over his food and drank too many Bintang beers.

At some point, we moved into the living room, most of the group around the couch admiring Isabel's first paper designs and the samples we were going to send to Indonesia for them to mass produce. Paul put "My Funny Valentine" on the turntable, "All Blues," Miles's transcendent horn. I'd seen him play it once, the trumpet painted partly orange, partly black, Miles in his dashiki all impulse and mentality and control. I stepped toward Jesse to buck him up, collect him into the fold, whispered in his ear about one of our secret angels, treating him to a taste of private information. Dennis Wilson was fronting us fifteen grand of capital, his piece was twelve percent. "Come on, Little Brother, tell me if you think a Beach Boy's going to back a loser. Dude survived the Manson Family, right? He's been hitting trifectas all his life."

Jesse took his time wrestling down the nugget—he seemed slugged into silence, and then he pinched out a little dribble of a smile, exasperated, naturally, but also more than a little bit impressed. "You know fucking Dennis Wilson?"

"Friend of a friend of a friend. He dug our samples, what can I say? But keep it to yourself. I think Izzy knew him way back when, and who knows if that memory is sweet. Look, everybody comes at this on a different tangent. For Bel, it's a shot at controlling her livelihood. My money guys see an easy buck or three. You and me, what we sell, the money, that's an excuse. It's the energy, slipping through the whirlwind together, seeing what falls to us if we do. Monday morning, put some ideas together about the physical operation, draft us a floor plan of how you want the store."

"I already have a job," Jesse said.

"Quit it. We do this with you running things or I'll bag the whole deal."

"And if you're wrong and there's no market? Times are shaky and some of us have more to lose than you."

I went over to the stereo, yanked the volume up. "Listen to the man play. You hear any lack of nerve? From the mind, to the heart, to the hand. That's what it takes to make something that matters, you just close your eyes and go."

Jesse looked at me. "I say yes and then what?"

"Who knows? That's the idea."

We stood there listening to the music, and I told Jesse it was better for things if he was the one who told Isabel about Dennis Wilson's contribution. Start himself off as the one in control. I watched him as he did as told, shaky on his pins at first, but smooth as champagne at the finish.

At Jesse's direction, they paint the store interior in baby greens and pale yellows—a palette chosen to trigger desire and acquisition. Lucy and her band of women carpenters put together beach-cabana dressing rooms and rough-sawn showcases that Jesse stencils with oversize tropical flora. On the wall behind the main sales counter he sketches the Hanuman logo five feet high. He spends days speckled with paint, giddy on the fumes. He paints the wall over twice to get the thing exactly right. Marty's been pushing him to goddamn finish, but Jesse stays the course. At last he's down to pesky details. He sets each hair on the monkey god's body with a glorious tick of his brush.

In the backroom, Isabel has been struggling at her design table in a silent clot of effort. It's up to Jesse to pull her out for a late night coffee or a dip into the ocean to clear her head, bring her takeout hot and sour soup or chile rellenos. He knows he should be nudging her to move more quickly, but he finds himself absorbed in watching her—how she bears down on her work, the density of her pencil line, the stern angle of her forearm on her pattern paper. Her torn-up drawings are in too many pieces to rescue.

For weeks Marty's been traveling the San Francisco-L.A. axis, booking newspaper ads and Yellow Pages listings, sniffing out private label accounts for a wholesale division. He's cherry-picked Isabel's address book for all her old connections—glam-rock costumers and Israeli consignment kings and Malibu wheeler-dealers. His dentists have fed the kitty thousands more in promissory notes.

Each night near midnight, the Hanuman phone rings and Jesse and Isabel receive the gush of Marty's optimism, the business he's corralled, the heavy hitters he's dined at Ernie's or Pips, the gross of Day-Glo Hanuman posters due in Santa Cruz a week from Tuesday, artwork bartered from a strung-out silkscreen maestro who did album work for Dylan and the MC5. All he wanted was a couch where he could catch some zees and four lids of Columbian skunk.

Later than they wanted, all the designs have flown their way to Bali, and Isabel relinquishes the conversation to Jesse. Her ear grazes the shared receiver; her breath is slow and polished by the scent of burnt orange. Marty expects good news only, so Jesse marches him through the day's triumphs, holds silent on how many Southern Comfort bottles he's fished out of Isabel's trash. After a while, almost in boredom,

Isabel pulls the receiver from Jesse, turns her back on him for low-voiced conversations that drift on into the night. Best to keep distance as he cleans his brushes and sweeps the floor, stalling with make-work so she won't be left alone in the empty shop. Isabel's voice murmurs below his hearing. She might be crying or laughing, Jesse can't decide.

By the middle of April, the store is coming together, but there's nothing in it to sell. Marty's got himself a blow-dried razor cut, a Goodwill business suit, a pair of used wingtips past their glory. He's generous with backslaps and praise for everyone's hard work. Once a week, he hands out paychecks, dishing them out like the jolly lord of the manor.

Jesse hasn't seen Isabel for a month—according to Marty she's making magic up in Felton by her lonesome, new designs more beautiful than anything they've dreamed about for shipment number two. He looks so bullish and radiant of eye, why couldn't it be so? Marty's never functioned with this much focus—no time anymore for pickup basketball or night-crawling after the essential sopaipilla. Work now, play later, he brings the hammer down.

Near the end of the month, Jesse takes a call from San Francisco, the goods are in. Time to drive up north and pick up the shipment from their customs broker, Rudy Moskowitz. In the empty storefront, the smell of paint still in the air, Marty explains the drill. Pay the broker his money, sign for the shipment, and drive their future home.

"Why me," Jesse asks. "What happened to the division of labor?"

"You're the guy. Don't fuss."

Jesse explains he still has plenty to do in Santa Cruz putting finishing touches on the store, organizing things for the arrival. Marty says all well and good, but it's Jesse has to go, he's on the paperwork, his name and Social Security number.

"Me? When did that happen?"

Marty's eyes soften in almost sympathy. He puts an arm around Jesse's shoulder, speaking slowly, as if explaining long division to a child. "Always was, Little Brother. Anyway, for me, duty calls. I'm going back to L.A. for another money-raising trip. I may have a line into Asylum Records. Fingers crossed, we could be doing Jackson Browne tour jackets come end of summer.

"Anyway, S.F.'s a milk run, Moskowitz will tell you what to do. Just follow the dots and all will be well. Course you might have to cut your hair and smile your little schoolboy smile. The man is *haimish* as the day is round, but I don't think he wants to be in business with the great unwashed."

"My hair is perfectly clean," Jesse tells him, but Marty's already across the room and dialing someone on the phone.

The broker's office is in the Ferry Building close by the Embarcadero, an overheated warren yearning for a paintbrush or a wrecking ball. For most of an hour, Jesse awaits Moskowitz's pleasure, alone in the musty anteroom, his hands clenched in his lap, his legs stretched out in front of him. Out on the sidewalk before coming in, he stuffed his ponytail inside his collar, but like a living creature, the thing threatens to leap free at any second.

The only reading material is a small wall calendar courtesy of the Chinatown Benevolent Society. It's the Year of the

Tiger, celebrated by an airbrushed nude on every page. Miss April cups her dainty breasts for the camera's eye. *Tigers are passionate and intemperate*, the caption reads. *They reject the authority of others.*

Moskowitz advances out of his office flashing a chunky gold wristwatch and matching ID bracelet. He gives Jesse a good going over—the faded Rep tie, the Frye boots needing a shine. The broker wears the all-purpose scowl of a fifty-five-year-old man whom nothing can surprise. He smells heavily of cloves.

"Jesse Kerf," the man says. "Hippie boots and the whole shebang. My kid has those shit-kickers, won't dress like a human even if I pay him. Follow me."

In his private office, Moskowitz lights a cone-shaped cigarette, clouding the air between them with the scent of a curry house. Jesse snaps opens his briefcase with what he hopes is professional éclat. "I'm told you're going to help us expedite our shipment in case we run into trouble at the dock."

"*Expedite*, nice. Me, I dropped out of school ninth grade, never made it up to 'expedite.' You're a college boy, aren't you, good for you, you got yourself a vocabulary."

"I dropped out," Jesse says.

Moskowitz grunts and pulls Jesse's documents out of a file folder. While the broker reviews the collection of manifests, bills of lading and invoices, Jesse deals several hundred dollar bills onto the desk. Hold your tongue and let the money sit in front of him, Marty instructed. Jesse watches the bills curl in the heat.

Moskowitz puts the papers aside and tips back in his chair for a thoughtful drag on his cigarette. "You look like a decent kid. You're a babe in the woods, O.K. everybody gets a first time. But don't insult me, if you don't mind? I got to reduce the blood pressure."

"It's not enough?"

"Christ, don't be a jerk-off. Here's some advice, no charge. Nobody pays cash anymore. My line, the green stuff makes everybody think too hard. I'm like a doctor or a plumber. I send you a bill—thirty days net. I take a bite for every entry on your list, a bigger one for every classification, messenger fees, it adds up. You send me a nice check, helps me put Janice and Larry through summer camp, buys me some more of these goddamn smokes, going to kill me before my time."

"Sorry, I guess I fucked up," Jesse says. "I'd been led to believe..."

Moskowitz interrupts him. "I got another piece of wisdom for you, sonny boy. A man in business—never apologize. Makes you look like you don't know squat."

Jesse listens as Moskowitz explains their deal in punishing detail, the man loving the chance to give instruction to the uninformed. Barring the unforeseen, his shipment will clear in forty-eight hours. Bring the papers to the U.S. Customs warehouse at the Oakland container terminal, and bring a truck, twenty-six footer should do it.

"For half a dozen crates of vests and bangles and masks? I was going to borrow a friend's VW bus."

Moskowitz rolls his eyes. "You read your docs, you've got eighty crates, almost thirteen hundred cubes. Fifty thousand doodads won't fit in a lousy hippie ride."

This is a mistake, Jesse wants to say, but the broker's strong hand is helping him toward the exit. Moskowitz makes a point of consulting his watch—there will be no fond good-byes. While the broker watches, Jesse shakes his hair out of his collar, fans it in relief against his shoulders. Just before he steps into the hallway, Jesse snatches up the Chinese calendar.

"So I don't forget to show up on the 29th," he tells the broker, sliding the pinups under his arm.

Outside, the salt air is bracing, the jolt of iodine promising life abundant. Come to think of it, fifty-thousand's the kind of number with Marty's name all over it. Jesse brings Miss April into the light. Her body shines in the spring sun as though catching fire.

NINETEEN

THE REGINA GRACE JOSTLES AGAINST PIER 59, lurching in the rain-struck water. Jesse steps out of his rented truck and watches a two-story crane jerk a container out of the ship's hold. Metal grinds against metal. The rain pours down. As the cargo hits the ground there's a wet thump, and three stevedores jump back to escape a shower of mud. Maybe it's the Hanuman shipment—fifty thousand lizard souls making their presence known. If Marty were here, he'd have something interesting to say about the view.

Moskowitz's call came at 8:30 this morning, the pier number barked into the receiver and the time the truck was needed at the port. Jesse knew better than to ask any questions.

"Got it," he said, and clicked off.

The customs shed smells of diesel and wet lumber and there are cartons and crates stacked everywhere as though lobbed willy-nilly by the storm. Heading for the office in the rear, Jesse negotiates the maze of aisles and half-aisles, dodging a silent forklift scuttling through the mess. The driver wears a hard hat with the Stars and Stripes over the brim. One look at Jesse's ponytail and dripping pea coat, and the driver's expression jells. Jesse pops him a sharp salute.

A large fellow in a bulky blue uniform manages the office, and he sits Jesse opposite him, inspects his papers while drinking a can of Coke. Every so often he turns to a ten-inch black-and-white TV that sits near him running without sound. In miniature, a newsman faces the camera on the roof of a building, palm trees in the distance, American soldiers behind him sitting in rows. It's raining there, harder than here, the raindrops whipped by helicopter wash.

"They won," the officer says, jabbing at the screen. Specks of cola spot a bill of lading, and Jesse wonders if he should snatch it to safety. The officer clutches his soda as though it is the dearest thing in the world. "We used to be a country to be proud of, but now I wouldn't give a bent nickel for the whole shooting match. You don't care, naturally, let Charlie wipe the floor with us, who cares."

Vietnam, Jesse finally puts it together. He hasn't been following the TV news or reading papers for more than a month. He's been in Marty-land—the timeless land of frog skins and flying monkeys with their tails on fire. "I think my waybills are all OK," Jesse says. "You'll tell me if I didn't dot my 'i's or cross my 't's."

The officer passes Jesse's sheaf of papers through his fingers, giving him a sideways look as he steps out of the room. On the TV set, soldiers jog into the belly of a helicopter. The picture's so tiny, nothing on the Marines' faces bleeds through the general blur.

Someone new walks into the office, and her navy skirt suit and neatly styled hairdo speak to a professional approach. She introduces herself as Special Agent Holloway, shows him her badge, and sits behind the desk, close enough for Jesse to smell her perfume, something woodsy. Holloway switches off the TV and dumps the Coke can in the trash.

"Name?"

Jesse tells her. As Holloway shuffles through the import documents, her jacket reveals a holstered gun under her arm.

"Mr. Kerf, you're in some serious trouble. I'm here to tell you you're under arrest."

She pulls a laminated card from her pocket and reads him his Miranda rights. Jesse finds himself grinning, as if treating things lightly will wind time back, make the moment evaporate into nothing. Holloway's stare betrays little. Thai stick, Jesse imagines, or hash, what they like to grow in Indonesia. Whatever Marty thought he'd smuggle in under Jesse's signature. His smile feels pasted on his lips.

"Somebody tell a joke I missed?" Holloway says. "Nothing about ten years in the feds seems all that funny to me. Violate 18 USC 545, we have a great desire to lock you away. Smuggling, in case you thought otherwise, is very much against the law."

Jesse finds his words cautiously. "I'm here to receive a shipment of Indonesian leather goods and crafts. Beyond that, I don't have a clue."

"Is that how you want to play it? Clueless? Why don't we have a little conversation, you and me. Maybe we can see what you do know."

"No," Jesse says. "Nothing more without a lawyer."

The customs agent pretends not to hear and tries to sell Jesse on the joys of confession. The court system, she promises, goes easy on any culprit disposed to save it time and dollars. Jesse clamps his jaw. The culprit, that curly-headed motherfucker, is God knows where. Maybe tooling along the Coast Road aiming for rain puddles and singing to the radio. Marty might be coming up on Castroville and stopping for a slice of artichoke pie.

Holloway finishes her pitch, clasps her hands together as though she's just delivered the Sunday homily.

"Excuse me," Jesse says, "You said something about pants?"

"The contraband, Mr. Kerf. Thirty thousand units of counterfeit blue jeans, right down to their copper rivets hiding under the leather and crafts you claim you're here for. Not the usual thing we see, sure, but highly profitable and as illegal as hell. Beautiful work, I might add, best I've ever come across."

"Blue jeans," Jesse says.

Holloway sighs. "You really want to play the idiot. We've got you on smuggling and trademark violations, just for starters. These are Class D felonies, maybe C once we figure out the street value. Levi's is the hometown brand in San Francisco, in case you forgot. The U.S. attorney's going to go for full extent, and we caught you dead to rights."

Jesse bites his lips, fighting off another smile. Fake blue jeans. It *is* a joke. "All news to me," he says. "Lawyer, please."

The woman sits back in her chair and tries to put on a friendly face. "Can I call you Jesse? OK, so maybe you're in the dark. A little lamb. Just a guy who showed up to carry the weight for someone else. It wouldn't be the first time. But then—this is hard to explain—yours is the only name on all the papers stretching from here to overseas and back. If there are other folks involved, just say the word. Your day will turn instantly better, I promise you."

Jesse shakes his head. "Do I get a phone call? Or is that just something they make up on TV?"

Inspector Holloway produces a pair of handcuffs. Her fingernails are short but neatly filed and polished red as roses. Jesse sticks out his wrists.

The boy was glowing by the time I bailed him out, fear, naturally, and anger, but something else surging through him, as though he'd mined up a new state of being. All that height, Jesse usually slumped down an inch or two when we were together, but going to the car, he stretched over me big as a tree. I couldn't keep up with him.

Once we were alone, he yelled and pounded his fist, furious because I'd sent him out blind, put him in harm's way without his say-so. I worried he was going to beat a dent in the dashboard or splinter a bone, but I admired all that unfiltered physical expression, his need to flush the venom out of his system. I wish I could've done more, but there were no good choices, only different kinds of bad. What was left was to guide him through the mess we were in. I saw a path to safety if Jesse wanted to take it.

We went to Wong's, a noodle place not far from the Bryant Street lock-up, the place done over like an antique railroad car, brass rails and plush banquettes, waiters dressed in Pullman porter military white. Midnight, and the place was humming with Chinese, Jesse and I the only Gwai-los in the joint. He ordered Chivas rocks and started in on me again, slapping the table with his palm, almost rattled the chow fun out of our bowls. Buck up, I told him, I'd already figured out a plan to make things right.

I showed him the headline in the Chronicle: SAIGON FALLS. "You heard the news? Hard to believe the time would ever come."

"You want to talk about Saigon?"

"Ho Chi Minh City. It's all over the radio, the NVA are repainting street signs as we speak. You got to love it, in the Twenties, Ho's a busboy at the Parker House, couple of trolley stops from where we lived. Now he's getting a city named after him, the father of his country. Fate rolls that way."

"So?"

"Tell me, Little Brother, you have any inkling when you were having breakfast, your day was going to hand you a shot to be a hero to your friends?"

Jesse was on his third scotch by now, and he was staring at me with that floaty look booze will give you, imagining, alas, his bust was something he and I were going to go through together. I hated to tell him I wanted him to keep the whole thing for his own, I had no choice.

Here was the rundown: we had an attorney on retainer who'd said he'd make book on Jesse's chances. A pink-cheeked first offender, lose the hair and dress him up in Hickey Freeman, he's the kind of defendant the jury wants to take home to fuck their daughter. The guy'd read Jesse's SAT scores into the record, truck in testimonials from his rabbi and his third-grade teacher, his heartbroken mom and dad. The very worst Jesse'd see would be three months' probation and a $10,000 fine that I'd dig up the scratch to pay. The point was the story began and ended with Jesse. It had to.

"I wish I could switch places with you and take you out of things entirely," I told him and I meant it. "It was my deal and I blew it royally—the jeans should have been buried under a bigger layer of goods, more hands greased, any number of angles I failed to predict. Believe me, the money was going to be astounding, make all of us whole forever. And the product, you should have seen them—501s so perfect even the Marlboro Man would put them on and never know."

Jesse was quiet, watching the raindrops smack against the window. I leaned forward in my chair. "But if this spreads beyond you, it will touch Isabel. She's got an old cocaine beef she never talks about, a parole violation, a chunk of history waiting to implode. She'll waste her thirties in Chowchilla. You take a plea, Jesse, play it like you were a one-man band and Customs will go to bed happy. We all will.

"You've talked to her about this?"

I didn't want to tell him it was her idea. "She won't be difficult," I said.

"You make it sound so figured out. All that's missing is a shiny ribbon."

"It's what we could jam together on short notice."

Jesse seemed strangely peaceful, sipped on his jasmine tea. "Now I know why your name is nowhere on any piece of paper. Just little old me."

I had to sigh. "No, man, it wasn't like that. I thought making you the number one would put some hair on your balls, bring you into your own. Sure, I had to keep a wall between me and my money guys and the rest of the show, but that was never the whole reason."

"Were they really that good?" he said.

"Was what?"

"The 501s. The customs agent said they were the best she'd ever seen."

I smiled. "She's got an eye. Don't usually find that in a cop."

Going home Jesse insisted on stopping to buy champagne. "We'll wake up everyone at Escalona House and drink a shout to Uncle Ho," he said. "The good guys won today."

In the late afternoon, Isabel jogs barefoot along the 26th Avenue beach, skirting the shoreline. Jesse watches from the cliff top as she churns past driftwood piles and tattered kelp without a thought for where she's putting her feet. If I went running, he thinks, where would I stop?

Isabel's turned into Little Ms. Health, Marty announced last night, three miles of running every other day and so long, coffee, so long, Southern Comfort, hello, Adele Davis. She's mixing brewer's yeast and bone meal into her morning muesli and juicing carrots by the carload. Last night, she didn't come down the mountain to Jesse's party, but spent three wan minutes with him on the phone while he shouted to her above the ruckus. They'd have dinner in the next few days, she promised, and was gone before he could ask her how she was.

At the breakwater, Isabel reverses direction and Jesse descends the stairs in time to her approach. Her face is tight with exertion and she hesitates when she sees him, running in place for a bit. Then she's back on pace, churning up sand. Jesse falls in next to her, fine to jog along in silence. Isabel stops, though, her body heaving. "You found me," she says after she's caught her breath.

"I didn't feel like waiting till tomorrow or next week or whenever. I've got room for a big workout, what about you, ready for more?"

She looks at him. "I don't like your pace."

She strips down and washes herself in the ocean while Jesse sits on dry ground. Her face tightens in a kind of grim pleasure as she douses herself with the freezing water. When Isabel returns to dress herself and sit next to him, Jesse can see how weary she is, dark circles under her eyes, her flesh pimpled with the cold. "I'm not going to throw myself at you and cover you with thankful kisses," she says. "That's not my style, but you know that, or you better. Is your mind made up?"

"Piece of cake," Jesse says. "Marty painted me the picture—I'll get a rap on the knuckles from some judge and then out the door into arms of my friends and lovers. Your tragic past is safe with me, don't worry."

"You're making fun. Fuck you." Isabel gets to her feet, but seems unwilling to move. She gazes down at him sadly. "Don't wring too much enjoyment from this, Jesse."

"Somebody's in a bad mood today. I thought it was me."

Isabel's laugh is bitter. "More than enough of that to share."

They walk together up the stairs to the parking lot and Isabel mounts her bike.

"Let me cook you dinner," Jesse says. "Adele Davis has an oatmeal loaf, I think."

The wind's picking up and fine sand powders their skin. Isabel puts out her hand to Jesse's face as if to brush him off and he leans close for her touch, receives instead a painful flick on his earlobe. "Don't know me so well," she says and stands hard on her pedals, leaving him alone.

Lulu's is two deep at the bar tonight and it's a fight for Jesse to order a sandwich and a row of boilermakers, solemnize the day with them—the drink of jailbirds and reprobates. There are women looking for dancing partners, but they look sideways at Jesse's sandy clothes and beery grin and pass him by. Hell, nothing wrong with swaying solo in the center of the dancing crowd, mug in one hand, shot glass in the other, sing along with the boleros—their lyrics nothing but tears and broken hearts. Beneath the mirror ball, the spinning lights map a picture Jesse can't unravel, follow the bouncing dots to where? Before the first tune ends, Lulu leads him to the door, where she kisses him on the cheek and orders him home.

Near midnight Jesse shows up in the alley behind Hanuman Designs, beer bottles tucked into his side pockets. He forces a window open—putting his shoulder to it—and the empty store is before him. It's bare from wall to wall and thick with the odor of Lysol and paint thinner. Gone the showcases, the thatched roof dressing rooms, gone the crates of T-shirts in the corner. Even Miss March has made an exit from her place near the front door. Someone's repainted the walls, the strokes of Jesse's mural blanked out in white primer, erased as if they never were. He crouches to the floor. Marty's eagle eye has skipped a spot or two: a few drops of magenta and yellow stain the polished wood.

Jesse scoots over to set his back on what had been the mural face and stretches out his legs and drinks a beer. He spins one of the empties on the floor, a rattle of glass on wood. Who could ever have seen this place as the repository of anybody's dreams? Empty, it seems smaller than before, ashamed of itself somehow. He finishes his second beer and stands unsteadily, finds his way outside to pee against the alley wall.

Around the corner, Jesse shivers at a pay phone waiting for his call to connect. The wind's blowing harder from the bay, salt in the air along with the scent of new roses. "Inspector Holloway," the voice announces at the other end at last.

"Jesse Kerf here. Just tell me where you want to meet, Ms. Holloway. I'm ready for that conversation." Jesse's breath mists the glass of the booth until his reflection vanishes.

TWENTY

1990

T<small>HE RESTAURANT BOLTED INTO VIEW</small> before Jesse was
ready for it. Bumper to bumper from the airport to Santa Monica, and it was all he could do not to dent the BMW.
Where was everybody going at 10:30 on a Sunday night?
Where had they been? The container of Marty's ashes shifted
on the passenger seat whenever Jesse was forced to slam on
his brakes.

At Copain, lights blazed and the front windows were open
to the weather, music sailing onto the street—Guns N' Roses
popping loud enough to summon the cops. He'd have to talk
to Cheryl. He could see her working the front of the house in
her leather skirt and famous fuck-me pumps, making sure the
servers hustled Helena's duck three ways and sashimi salad to
the customers. Cheryl was the best manager and sommelier
they had—she'd polished the art of ego massage in rehab. If
you can put one over on your fellow junkies, she once told
him, you can con a deuce of Hollywood morons into buying
the $120 cabernet.

On the patio, mushroom heaters loomed over the tables,
and the faint smell of propane moved on the breeze. It was
a cool night, but even in February Jesse's patrons required
access to the out-of-doors. Stopped near the parking valet,
he watched a four-top toasting each other with a round of

margaritas. The waiter had lit the triple sec on fire before setting down the glasses: a blue flicker licked up at the tanned, eager faces. No one hesitated to drink.

Jesse took the car to the back alley, tucked into the lot next door so as not to be seen at the restaurant's rear entrance. The kitchen noises made him grit his teeth—the crash of pots and pans at the sink, the busboys roaring at a joke in Spanish. It had been five days since he'd flown the red-eye to Boston to shut down the Somerville apartment and manage Marty's death. Jesse's clothes smelled of mildew; everything he owned was damp and caked with cobwebs and dust. Only Marty's Luccheses had weathered the trip in good order—the boots molded to Jesse's feet as though they'd been made for him.

He squinted at Marty's watch in the darkness. As he expected, on the dot of 11:15 Helena came out for her nightly smoke. Her whites were grease-stained and her baseball hat was fingerprinted with gravy. She looked in her standard fury, blew smoke through her nostrils, one hand balled into a fist. Six years before, they'd gotten married in a fit of lustful optimism. They'd put a good face on it for ten months, most of the time spent in bitter silence or in bed. Finally, they'd had the sense to call it quits.

Helena squashed her cigarette to the ground and stomped back inside. Jesse could hear her howl at the pastry chef over a less than perfect chocolate soufflé. What would she do if Jesse told her about Marty and the apartment and the InfoCon millions—would she tuck him into her arms or speed-dial the accountant? He pulled the car onto the street and drove north for home. Up Temescal, where he lived, the night-blooming jasmine would be spreading its scent.

It wasn't until the BMW came to the light at Zuma that Jesse realized he'd missed his turnoff fifteen minutes back. German automotive luxe: the sedan was driving itself. Fog was descending, the dense winter fog California specialized in, the kind responsible for three or four fatalities a year.

As his headlights cut through the mist, the cliffs of Point Mugu shone out of the murk. LAX was probably socked in; he'd made it down by a few hours' grace. Jesse eased the car through the tight curve around the point, then punched it hard for the straightaway. He could drive all night, he thought, and make Santa Cruz by morning.

Near dawn, he broke the journey in Soledad, ordering coffee at a truck stop off 101. He was alone in the place and the waitress fussed near him while she sponged the counter and rearranged the pies. She wore her pink uniform too snugly, one of those people who'd made it to her thirties overspending in flesh and emotion. She was in a mood to talk about her boyfriend Marlon; his faithless ways had done her dirt more times than she wanted to know. Carlie was her name—Carlie and Marlon, destiny had brought them together, she said, their names so close. Sometimes you're in clover, Carlie had the opinion, sometimes you're in shit, pardon her French. How do you tell the difference, Jesse wanted to ask.

A young local came in, a farmhand in his twenties who wore a black Stetson and a touring jacket for the rock band Poison.

"Hey there, Roddy," the waitress said and poured him a mug of coffee. Roddy grunted and sat himself three seats away. His hair, Jesse noted, was a blond so white it must have been dyed. Roddy twirled his legs around the stool with the physical confidence of a natural athlete.

"Lookin' at something, mister?"

"Sorry," Jesse said.

"Keep it up, I'll dust your fucking pinhead off."

Carlie glided over. "How about a nice sticky bun, honey," she asked Roddy. "Raisins and cinnamon and lots of that sugar glaze. Just made fresh—still warm from the oven."

"Dude was looking at me. Shouldn't stare at somebody, it ain't right. L.A. faggot. That your faggot car, faggot?"

Jesse felt a surge—perhaps a fight was exactly what he needed, better for the system than caffeine. "Why don't you talk politely in front of the lady," he said. "Mind your manners and your mouth."

Carlie came around the counter and put herself between the men and laid a calming hand on the younger one's arm. "You just forget about him, we don't need to worry about somebody we don't know. Come on over to a booth and I'll get you that roll." Roddy shot Jesse a final carnivorous glare, but let himself be pointed to a far corner of the restaurant.

"Now, do you need something sweet to settle you down, too? I'm giving out free samples this morning," Carlie asked Jesse. He told her no.

"Thanks for sticking up for me," she said. "It was kind of wasted on Roddy, though."

Jesse tossed a few dollars on the counter. "Maybe you should have let him knock me around—I bet you could use a little excitement in your shift." He took himself to the john to wash his face. His legs were shaking, he discovered. What would it take to be the one accounted a threat?

Roddy was gone when Jesse passed through the café and Carlie was nowhere to be seen, replaced by a woman in her sixties who ignored him as he went out to the parking lot. The sunrise had burnt off the fog, and in the distance, a hawk circled above the valley, harrying its prey. They mated for life—Marty had taught him that, one of the thousand things he knew.

The BMW, when he came to it, looked wrong. Someone had keyed the paint on almost every panel. Nails stuck out of both rear tires, and on the driver's seat, a squashed cinnamon roll dripped over the leather. Jesse edged back and found a place to sit and consider the scope of the damage.

"You all right over there?" It was Carlie going home, puffed out in a down parka. She wheeled a rusty moped.

"Your friend Roddy's got quite a talent."

Carlie took in what had happened to the BMW and offered to call the deputy. Jesse pictured himself in the local police station, listening to the banter of the cops and signing his name to forms for the rest of the day. "Don't bother," he said, and yanked his duffel bag out of the trunk. The carton with Marty's ashes was still on the passenger's seat, miraculously intact. He stuffed it inside the bag.

"What's your name," Jesse asked. Carlie didn't answer.

"Your name, Carlie, your last name?"

"Davis, how come?"

Jesse found what he wanted in the glove compartment and scribbled with a pen, shoving the paper toward her. The pink slip, signed over. "Here. Car's yours. Fill in the rest yourself."

The waitress backed away. "You're crazy."

"So what? It's a BMW. Everybody wants one, it's the

best driving machine in the world. Don't you watch the commercials?"

"Why don't you let me call the deputy," Carlie said.

Jesse crushed the pink slip into her hand. "Do me the favor, Carlie. How much could it take to get it into shape, a few hundred dollars? Give me your address and I'll send you whatever it costs. Think how Marlon will walk the straight and narrow, his girlfriend speeding around in her very own 520i."

"Why are you doing this?"

Jesse hoisted up his belongings, and the stiff muscles of his shoulders gave a crack. "A friend of mine once said, everything happens for a reason. Let's leave it at that."

As he hiked up the on-ramp, the draft from a passing semi blew him against the safety rail. Jesse regained his place and stuck out a thumb. He could wait as long as it took.

There's Jesse now, poking around the house on Escalona, knocking on doors and peeking through windows. Nobody's home, Little Brother, it's a working day, the old folks putting a dollar in their pockets and the little ones in school. The house hasn't changed, has it, that ugly yellow paint we lifted from a storage locker over at U.C., the posters for Earth First and Nicaragua, the macramé shades? Christ, it brings me back. Something fine in remembering who we once were.

Paul and Natalie—decades on and look at them, holding the line, toiling for the voiceless and the poor and the oppressed. Tyranny's a growth business these days, no shortage of the iron hand and many reasons to lose faith. But our old roommates have stayed on course, they've kept their hearts pure. More than me. More than most. They've got two kids, I wonder if you heard.

Hey, Jess, the sign you painted over the door, old Uncle Ho, he's faded now, but there he is still banging in the wind. I'm glad nobody ripped it down after your foxtrot with the feds. Some wanted to—they were angry, claimed they didn't know you anymore, or never did. Turning state's witness was a bigger crime than mine, some said. But I argued no, you were pressed beyond your limits and you lacked the necessary limberness to bend. A failure of biology, not character, not will.

I wished you'd stuck around instead of turning tail for Santa Monica. That was where you let us down, fear running you instead of nerve. You should know I did my year point five in Lompoc standing on my head. I didn't waste my time, and I learned a trick or two. And so did you. And so will you again.

Right, it comes back, doesn't it—the key's stashed under the avocado plant, a taste of illegal entry, very much to the old standard. There's our couch, that musty green corduroy, what wars it's seen. Go on, lie down and catch yourself some shut-eye, you need the rest. You look poured out. Grief does that—redecorates your soul. Don't worry, Paul and Natalie should be glad to see you and sniff around the past. They don't know you've got some news that's going to bring them down. My advice is don't be bashful; say it straight. Dead is dead.

Afterward, I suggest a stroll around downtown. You missed it coming in. There was an earthquake last year—maybe you forgot. The Big One, or almost, there were tremors from mid-coast to San Francisco. The town's been smacked around. The Garden Mall's a field of broken brick and glass, and there are temporary bubble buildings everywhere you turn, and painted banners sticking a pretty face over the destruction.

They say it's going to take a decade to rebuild. The longer the better—ten years might be too short for everyone to understand the story. We're small and the universe is big. It moves just how it likes. We think if we keep nosing along, we'll stumble up against the meaning, glimpse something of the ultimate design. I wish I could say there was one. You know me, I went for moment to moment. The only plan, if you want to call it one, was the food chain. Everybody ends up dinner on somebody else's plate.

The argument woke him up. Paul and Natalie were in the kitchen from the sound of it and someone was cooking supper—onions and garlic and tomatoes, the garlic wanting a gentler hand. They were keeping their voices down but Natalie's familiar animation refused to be corralled. Fuck nostalgia, I want him gone, Jesse heard her say.

Exhaustion prickled beneath Jesse's eyelids, a hard crust of fatigue. He could do this, he thought—tell them and then take off. It wouldn't be what Marty would like, a minimum of weeping and lamentation, but Marty had no vote. Jesse sat up to look for the box of ashes.

The boys of the house were camped out on the stairs. They kept their eyes on him as though instructed to call an alarm when he awoke. The older one was ten or so; he had Natalie's dark good looks and a nervous manner with his hands on the stair rail. The six-year-old had put on Jesse's boots. "Are you a real cowboy?" the boy asked. "Dylan said no way."

Jesse swung his legs down to the floor and spiked his foot on something sharp—a plastic robot or car, he couldn't tell. "Anybody can have a pair of boots. I've never been on a horse or even a pony. My name's Jesse. What's yours?"

"Don't tell him," the older boy said. He whacked his brother instructively on the head and the little one jumped into it and hit him back. They fought like small animals, slamming their bodies in all directions. They were having fun, Jesse decided. He left them where they were and limped to the kitchen.

Natalie was rushing through her chores, laying out the supper dishes and keeping half an eye on the stove. The years had treated her well—filled her out and settled her to ground. In her tailored wool outfit, she looked ready for anything. She was a lawyer, Jesse recalled, immigration and labor on the angels' side. She was setting four places at the table.

Paul grabbed Jesse on sight and kissed him on both cheeks, spun him around and wouldn't let him go. He was plumper than Jesse remembered but he was light on his feet and his face welled over with pleasure as he led Jesse on a tour of the house. Paul talked rapid-fire, as though trying to squeeze the last fifteen years into the first three minutes.

The impression was of clutter and making-do, the ceilings cracked and peeling, the rooms and hallways piled up with broken tools and bicycles and stacks of LPs. Jesse's former bedroom had become a catch-all for boxes of yellowing photographs and handbills and other ephemera. Its walls were marbled with dust, and clothing and toys were tossed around as though someone had fled the house in panic. Jesse stood in the midst of it without moving. It was a minute or more before he could remember where he'd had his bed.

"Gotta bring you back," Paul said. "A trip and a half."

Jesse sidestepped a bundle of twenty-year-old concert posters from the Shoreline Amphitheater. "You ever want to cash in on some of this, I know some collectors in L.A."

Paul looked shocked. "Why would I want to sell? I like my stuff."

"Just thinking about your bottom line. A little money in hand and you could afford a cleaning service, get things more in control."

"Like there's a universe where Natalie would hire a maid. You shouldn't have been such a stranger, man. You've lost track of how we live."

Jesse's face reddened. "If there was an open invitation, somebody forgot to tell me. That wasn't exactly a hero's welcome I got from Nat."

Paul shrugged as though to make allowances for his wife's lack of welcome. "You're here now. Stay for supper, stay longer. The more the merrier."

"OK," Jesse said. "But if Nat wants me gone, I'm gone."

They squeezed around the table and ate spaghetti and talked about the dinners Escalona House had hosted—the one with the drunken Belgian director who kept shouting how cinema was revolution rendered concrète, while attempting footsie with Lucy under the table. Jesse did the accent and Natalie laughed and the children too, and it seemed for a while as though everything that needed to be forgotten would drift away.

The boys had ice cream and went off to watch TV. Jesse retrieved the Blanton's from his duffel bag and served out some of Marty's good bourbon. It was time, as reasonable as any, and he told them about the accident. Paul blanched and he reached for Natalie. She leaned against him, blinking back a rush of tears. Jesse felt his eyes pooling—he was a little tipsy, enough to start them through the turns that began with Mrs. Folari's phone call. Almost at once, though, Paul left the room.

"Is this too hard for him?" Jesse asked Natalie. "I didn't think he really liked Marty."

She shook her head. "No, no, he's gone for Dylan and Zach. He thinks whatever we hide from them will come and get them in their thirties. He doesn't want them to have to shell it out for therapy."

Paul nudged the two boys into the room and he and Natalie took one each on their laps and Jesse began again. He repeated the highlights, Marty in his casket, the empty InfoCon office, Marty's sixty thousand dusty books. He didn't have the energy to talk about the money and left it for another time, capping things instead with a description of the incident with the BMW. He painted himself the clown.

"You're kidding, right?" Natalie said. "This is a joke—a $30,000 car?"

"Forty-five," Jesse said.

"Forty-five, pardon me. You junk it like it's litter?"

"Something like that."

Natalie got up to take the boys to bed. A vein skittered in her neck. "You and Marty, you're two peas. Everything's bullshit to you. Try running a real life sometime."

"Mommy said a dirty word," Zach said as he followed her out of the room.

Jesse looked at Paul. "Marching orders, it seems to me."

"Nah, she's over the edge on everything right now. I just ignore her. You know I had a record store? We had an earthquake in October and the place got walloped. That's been hard on Nat. Captain Analog, vinyl only. We're reopening in a month or two, bigger and better than before. We're gonna be great—digital's a dead end, anyone with ears can tell you that."

Paul told Jesse to bunk wherever he liked and went up to kiss his boys goodnight. In the living room, the terrain was more or less familiar. Yes, there were toys and children's books everywhere, and the record collection had swollen beyond counting, but the shadows fell as Jesse remembered and the couch would do for now. The sounds of childish temper filtered down the stairs, and what appeared to be the stomp of the Luccheses on the bedroom floor. A real life, Natalie had called it.

TWENTY-ONE

At breakfast, Paul worked on Jesse to stay another week. The sheetrock had recently gone up at Captain Analog, and there was a spot by the main sales desk perfect for a mural, a Kerf original. Their logo was a pirate—eye patch and parrot, but Paul couldn't stop thinking that they had to redo him using Marty's face. Natalie had her back to them making school lunches at the kitchen counter, and Jesse watched her shoulders tighten under the fabric of her blouse. But the idea had a poetry that he didn't want to deny. He went to Natalie and put a hand on her sleeve, offered to finish for her so she could take some time for herself before she went to work. Natalie's eyes were over-bright from lack of sleep and she stared at Jesse, then slid the knife and bread toward him. "Dylan won't touch his sandwich if you don't cut off the crusts," she said and went to gather her boys for school.

Painting the mural took four days. Astonishing how the design poured out of him, as if he'd stashed it away and only had to dredge up what he wanted from memory. Jesse drew Captain Analog as a basketball player, lent him Marty's hooked nose and something of his crooked grin. Instead of a ball, he set an LP between the character's outstretched fingers and arched the figure on its toes, poised for a jump shot. It captured Marty in a moment of becoming: his impatience, his endless requirement for motion. A decent likeness, better than Jesse imagined.

At both ends of the day, he jogged the route between Escalona House and work—an old discipline he saw no need to change. He had the streets mostly to himself. The few people he passed were stubbornly cheerful; they cleaned windows and watered window boxes as though every homely chore would rub the earthquake from remembrance.

The majority of downtown was boarded up or tumbled to pieces; the inflatable shopping pavilions billowed in the wind as if they were about to drift to sea. He would finish the painting, he thought, and never come back.

In the afternoons Jesse made a point to clean up early and cook supper for the household. Paul and Natalie's boys had decided to befriend him and they stood on footstools and helped at the counter, the three of them wearing white chef's aprons and toques Jesse'd picked up downtown. Spaghetti carbonara and Cajun meatloaf and kung pao shrimp—dishes Jesse learned in this very kitchen at Marty's elbow. Zach and Dylan were good students. What he was teaching them would serve them forever.

He avoided calling the restaurant, let them trudge on without him, but the afternoon he completed the mural, Jesse went out to stretch his legs and found himself at a phone booth, feeding in dimes and waiting for the ring. The other end opened onto a barrage of rock-and-roll. "Turn down the goddamn music, Cheryl," he kept shouting into the receiver until the volume receded a hair and she came on.

"The long lost Jesse Kerf. You forget where we were? Got a pencil, I can give you the address."

"Very funny. Find some other music to inflict on the lunch crowd, sweetheart. AC/DC will curdle the crème brûleé."

"We aren't doing crème brûlée anymore. Which you'd know if you hadn't dropped out of the world."

According to the Times, Helena's crème brûlée was worth a forty-minute drive; they'd had it on the menu since day one. "Jesus," Jesse said. "Go to the kitchen and tell her to pick up."

"She's out," Cheryl said. "Everybody's out, I've been humping nothing but five-sixes, it's a wonder I'm still here. Manuel's running the show, it's a thing of beauty, drop by sometime and see for yourself. You are coming home, boss?" Her plaintive tone was a novelty. What would be next— Cheryl in Laura Ashley?

Across the street, a wrecking ball chewed another piece from a Victorian storefront; Jesse tasted the brick dust in his throat. "I'll be there any minute," he told her. "Sooner than you want." He cut the connection and watched the wrecker finish its work.

Tonight the boys demanded Jesse for story time, and after they had heard their chapter and were tucked in, he walked down to the lanai for a hot tub. Natalie had gotten there before him and was drinking a glass of wine. She watched Jesse take off his clothes, then shut her eyes. Chlorine-scented mist drifted between them.

He eased into the tub—it was an old wine cask—and ducked under the surface, rose and shook the water through his hair. On one side of his head, his hair was clotted with dried paint. He used to love that feeling, the sense that work had left its measure on his body.

"I thought you and Paul were going to play records," Natalie said.

Paul was on a buying run, hot for a collection of Springsteen bootlegs, they'd listen later or tomorrow. Natalie hoisted up and sat on the edge of the tub. She'd rebuilt herself at the gym, a concentration of muscle and bone with a C-section scar tracking palely beneath her pubic hair. Naked, she seemed less vulnerable than clothed, if that were possible— trim and battle hardened. She put on her robe and looked down at him, how he imagined she drew a bead on witnesses in court.

"There's something I want you to do," she told him.

"Name it."

"Go home. You've finished your painting, so go back to your restaurant and your fancy meals and your Hollywood clientele. We used to be friends, Jesse. Old times should count for something."

"I thought we were feeling simpatico. Or pretending to."

"Is that what they taught you in L.A., how to pretend? Look around you—we can hardly crawl from one end of the week to the other without you hanging around confusing things. Have you completely forgotten what it takes to stay connected to what you believe?"

"Dylan and Zach will forget me twenty minutes after I'm out the door. Next week it will be comic books and go-carts or Mao's little red book if that's what you want."

The moon had risen and its pale, gray light planed the edges from Natalie's features. "You really don't have a clue.

It's Paul who's in danger, Paul you'll drag down. This morning he got the bright idea he wants to grow the business, you can help him get a toehold in Santa Monica. He's drowning with the little he has. We won't survive."

"You should give Paul more credit," Jesse told her. "Maybe he could bring it off." He got out of the tub and toweled dry and put on his clothes. Natalie followed him into the kitchen.

"Do I have to beg you?"

"I like it better when you're issuing instructions. More familiar."

Natalie laughed and her face opened to him. "If you want to win your cases, you learn to hit your marks."

The tub had flooded color to her cheeks—all that spirit, she probably still showed Paul a run for his money in bed.

"Marty left me an inheritance," Jesse said. "A little over $8 million. I want you and Paul and the boys to have some of it. I'm sure it would make Marty happy if he knew."

Natalie's hand jerked to the collar of her robe; for a while she didn't speak. "You won't be satisfied until you ruin us," she said at last.

"What are you talking about? I just want to spread around some good fortune."

There were tears in her eyes. "Is that what you call it?"

She waited until he gave her his promise to say nothing to Paul, then went upstairs. Jesse put some music on and sat for a while in the living room drinking the last of the Blanton's. A celebration of fucking up in every way at every turn.

It didn't take long to pull together his few belongings. The Lucchese boots were in Zach's room and Jesse was about to carry them off when the boy stirred in his sleep. Jesse bent to give him a kiss; the kid smelled of garlic from tonight's pesto genovese. He left the boots in their place and went downstairs and finished packing. He wanted a look at Marty's portrait before he left.

Paul drove up while Jesse sat on a downtown bus bench waiting for the San Jose airport van. He bounded out of his car but stopped short, looking a bit sheepish to have played detective. Paul had something in a paper bag, which he moved from hand to hand like a bashful suitor. "Who said you could split without saying goodbye?" he said.

Jesse smiled. "The quick fade, a specialty of the house, don't take it personally. What's that you're hiding over there? Not a bon voyage present, I hope."

It was the cardboard container of ashes. "You forgot Marty," Paul said, putting the box into Jesse's hands. "I didn't know what to do with him."

The thing sat on Jesse's lap, slightly tattered around the edges. "Like anybody ever did," he said.

Paul wanted to drive Jesse to the airport, and they sputtered up the hill. The ancient Saab was a pint-size version of the house: a repository of record albums and thrift shop refuse glowing with a comfortable aroma, part pepperoni pizza, part old clothes. Jesse burrowed in, throwing whatever was in his way into the back and laying the ashes box on top. Paul was right to track him down, no telling when they would see each other again.

When they came up to High Street, Jesse asked Paul to turn, and he complied with a sideways glance—they both knew it was 17 to San Jose, not 9. The signs pointed them to Felton. "We'll take the route through the trees," Jesse said. "I'd like a look at the redwoods. We have the time."

Paul shook his head with brotherly concern. "You aren't thinking she still lives there, Jesse? I mean, nobody's heard diddly-boo from her in years and years, not since she vanished just before the trial. I bet going up there isn't such a good idea."

"Probably isn't," Jesse said. "Let's do it anyway."

Nothing about Isabel's road came back to him; most of the houses had been repainted and added on to, and one entire stretch of woods had been developed into a cul-de-sac of cheap duplexes dotted with fiberglass spas and two-year-old trees. Jesse found himself looking down at his lap more than out the window.

Paul had come to the opinion that setting eyes on Isabel's former cabin would be cathartic for Jesse and kept asking where they should stop. There were three or four it could be, and Jesse settled on one to bring the question to a halt. It was shingle-style like hers had been, set back from the road, but the driveway was straight where hers had been curved, and there were too many doors and gables. The Saab's headlights whitened a small side deck that held a swing set and a tricycle and two potted geraniums.

Jesse brushed fog off the window glass and tried to arrange what he saw into something better shaped to his recollection. An electronic glow battered a downstairs casement—someone changing channels one after the other. They could be anywhere.

He turned away. "Come on, let's go before somebody calls the cops."

"We just got here."

"I don't need any more," Jesse said.

At the airport drop-off, they parted awkwardly, Paul hanging onto Jesse for dear life as a red-cap snatched at the duffle. Jesse watched Paul trot through the parking lot, pausing at every row. He'd misplaced the car, but he walked lightly, as though he didn't care.

TWENTY-TWO

J ESSE'S PLACE WAS CANTILEVERED over the canyon walls.
Built in the early sixties by a student of Richard Neutra, its
right angles and floor-to-ceiling glass were a placid argument
for the boundless American prospect. Jesse decorated it with
furniture by Saarinen and Eames and had the rooms painted
four barely distinguishable tones of gray. The painters redid
their work twice before he was satisfied.

There were more than thirty messages on his answering
machine. He set down his duffle bag and counted the flashes—
3 in the morning, who'd want an answer now? Helena might
be awake but she'd be screwing her new boyfriend, Charles.
That was always on the bill in the wee hours after the restaurant closed—and woe to the man who failed to deliver.

He found the box with Marty's ashes, gave it a dusting and
stuck it on the mantel. That was how it was done—turn the
thing into bric-a-brac, make it vanish into the general scheme.
He switched on his stereo and Schubert piano shone through
the room. Brendel's magisterial touch on the Impromptus:
the music of petticoats and duels under the plane trees. Jesse
opened the doors and stood on his balcony while the melody
played. It would rouse the coyotes and the neighbors, but fine,
let it roll down the canyon. He stood there and traced the fall of
earth toward the highway and the distant lights of the pier and

the dark ocean beyond. The carousel was still spinning—an endless revolve in every color of the rainbow. He watched until the Schubert ended and then went to bed.

In the morning, he poured himself a glass of guava juice and did the laundry and opened mail, sorted the bills. Then he called Helena to tell her Copain was going to have to miss him for a little while longer. She was on her treadmill as she took the call, panting as he stumbled through an explanation. His personal business still hanging him to dry. She didn't ask for details and took his excuses more calmly than he expected. She told him to do what he had to—they'd carry him until he was ready to come back. Helena's voice drifted away, as if she was already onto the next thing on her list but had forgotten to click off.

"One of these days we'll have a heart-to-heart," Jesse said.

"Of course we will." She picked up running again and they said goodbye over the pounding of her equipment. She'd have the lawyers all over their partnership agreement before the week was done. You could bank money on it.

He switched on the Brendel again and took a shower, leaving the bathroom door open to the music, then called a travel agent. Five flights to Maui today—the first would put him on the ground before dinner with an hour in a car to Lucy's house. He had never been to Hawaii before, and all he could think of was hula dolls and rayon shirts and mini-bar macadamia nuts. Lucy was pregnant now, well along with it. Seeing her would put his mind to happier times. Jesse drank the last of the guava juice and licked his lips. So sweet it gave him a headache.

The ride to Lucy's went past pineapple groves and condo developments and the foothills that rose in the lee of the volcano. The light was changing, the light after sunset, a dense, electrified blue that threw everything into relief. Drizzle had started, but Jesse kept his window open. The rain stirred up a ripe, green scent.

At Ho'okipa he stopped at an overlook where he could watch the wind-surfers in the bay. In the fading light, five of them breasted the rollers, flipping head over tails in whipsaws of neon-colored sail before they glided to shore. Jesse gazed out his windshield—how many years since he'd been in the water? Maybe he'd give it a try before he returned home.

Lucy's instructions led him down a rutted dirt road designed for four-wheel drive. The last hundred yards, Jesse abandoned his rental and slogged through the rain on foot. The house was set into a clearing; it was small and constructed of quirky gables and curves and a potpourri of mismatched windows and carved doors. The rain made music on its metal roof.

Lucy and her girlfriend, Eileen, waited for him on the porch safely out of the weather. They lay together on an old settee, and at first Jesse thought they were talking. No, Eileen was reading from a book, casting light on the pages with a candle lantern. Lucy listened with closed eyes, one hand curled over the dome of her belly. It was *Lord of the Rings*, Lucy's favorite, he remembered, a world of spells and dragons and place names with more consonants than they could hold. He shifted his duffle to his other shoulder and moved forward slowly. "Got any room up there for an old, wet man?" he said.

Lucy kissed him and marched him inside to dry him off while Eileen made dinner in the kitchen alcove. Lucy seemed unchanged by the approach of childbirth, a spike-haired sprite from her storybook with a basketball-size midsection as a minor addendum. She couldn't remember how long it had been since they'd last been together.

"Sixteen years," Jesse told her. Lucy had a long, appraising look at him and his face got hot.

"Been some ups and downs along the way," she said. She moved around him and bumped him accidentally with her belly. Jesse wanted to lay his cheek on it, test its firmness, its quality of life. "I have something to tell you," he said. "Bad news."

"No shit. I didn't think you hopped over here to work on your tan."

"Marty died two weeks ago—a car accident."

Lucy refused to flinch. "Holy fuck. So you were hooked back with him, kissed and made up? That must have been a little wonder of a conversation. Wish I could have been there."

"I haven't talked to him since Santa Cruz," Jesse said, while tears ran down his cheeks. Lucy let him have his cry.

He brought out the box of Marty's ashes to keep them company, and he and the women stayed up late trading stories about the man at his worst. The news of the inheritance barreled out of him, and Lucy chuckled when Jesse wondered if they'd accept some of the haul. She tapped her drowsy girlfriend on the shoulder. "Man wants to know if we're too high-and-mighty for a piece of Marty's stash?"

Eileen was a small woman like Lucy, though thicker in the body, yet there was a gracefulness about her and a wellspring of sweet nature as though the world had yet to do her wrong.

She looked at Lucy to be sure she wasn't joking, and said, "We'd be dumb not to, I guess —diapers and music lessons, college, even. We could give some of it to charity."

By midnight it was decided that Jesse should camp out in the guest room as long as he wanted. He was family, Lucy said, and whatever went down once upon a time, she wasn't in the mood to pick over the bones. She patted her abdomen. "Only thing of interest in this neighborhood is the mysterious future. Why don't you cool out for a while and see what shakes."

"If my partner hasn't sold me down the river, I have a business to run and a life in L.A., important obligations."

"Nobody has a life in L.A. Only a collection of events and people and recently acquired objects." She pointed out the window to the moonlit flank of Haleakala rising in the distance. "Walk through the crater at sunrise and then we'll talk about what's important and what's not."

"A few days," Jesse said. "That's all I have."

He did what he could to fit in. In a backyard wood shop, Lucy and Eileen ran a business turning salad bowls and candlesticks out of tropical hardwood. Jesse offered to reorganize the accounts, which were a bungled mess. The chore was refreshingly simple-minded. Often, he'd look up from his desk to the women at their lathes. They held their chisels against the Koa blocks with remarkable control, paring the raw wood into something beautiful and of use. The sawdust dyed their air-masks, skin, and clothes a deep burnt red, as if they were carved out of the same stock.

Mornings before breakfast, Jesse weeded the side garden, winging rocks into the brush until his arm ached. The plot sprawled with anthurium and heliconia, and he chopped the flowers back with everything he had, wrestling what was left into well-behaved patches. He filled the house with blooms.

After lunch he put aside his ledger books and drove to the surfers' beach for a sprint along the water line, followed by a plunge into the shallows. The ocean was bluer than he had ever known, the sun hotter, the sky lit from within. Maybe he *had* come here for the tan.

One afternoon when Jesse returned from his run, Eileen was at the woodpile, carving a cradle out of a log of Norfolk pine. The swing of her adze tossed shaved wood behind her in a quick, scented arc. Lucy watched from a rocking chair on the porch, and Jesse sat beside her, admiring Eileen's skill. They ate some passion fruit plucked from Lucy's vines.

"If this isn't heaven, I don't know what is," he told Lucy. "Everything you need in arm's reach, including someone to love. If I were you I'd never leave."

Lucy licked her fingers. "You haven't heard us fight."

"Aren't you happy together?"

"Yeah, but we don't make a pop song out of it."

"I'm what, too romantic, that's what you're saying? I've got my head in the clouds?"

Lucy cut into the fruit, exposing its bright black and yellow center. "It's not a crime."

Jesse listened to the blunt stroke of Eileen's tool against the wood. "I'm not sure Marty would agree." He went into the house to wash the juice from his skin.

The night turned hot and the breeze flocked the screens with insects and the perfume of moon flowers. Jesse slept fitfully. Only a few hours later, he jolted awake, twisted in his sheets. Lucy was sitting on his bed, calmly playing a flashlight beam against his face as if that were standard at 4 in the morning. No griping—zero hour had come, time to visit the volcano. He could get there before sunup and be home for dinner if he hustled the eleven miles in and out of the summit. It would change how he looked at everything. Jesse hid under his blanket—he needed sleep, he told her, not a self-improvement project.

Lucy peeled back the covers. "You don't know what you need."

She watched him put on sneakers, hurried him down her lane and tucked him into the car, told him how to find the summit road. She reached through the side window and set his palm atop her navel. "Feel that, the little señor had his Wheaties today, he's doing back flips."

Sure enough, an elbow or foot rippled within the drum of her belly, amazingly strong—he'd never felt anything like it. Jesse spread his fingers to take in more of the sensation. "You're having a boy," he said.

"Tell me about it. But you'll be hanging out here, I bet, now that you know the way? Watch football with the kid, and play trucks, show him how to whiz standing up?"

"I can teach him how to make a tarte tatin."

In the dim light, he could just pick out Lucy's faltering smile. She seemed tired and afraid —the mysterious future hurtling toward her faster than she knew.

"Hey," Jesse said. "You'll sail through this, you and Eileen. You'll be a family. That's what you want."

"The expert speaks. And you—what do *you* want?" Her knuckles were white against the window frame.

"Well," Jesse told her. "Wouldn't it be great if I knew?"

He drove in darkness toward the highlands. A ramble through a dead volcano, fine. And then back to California. Time to go home.

Knowing what to want—it's not exactly Jesse's talent, is it? Always stalling for a perfect unison of place and time, weighing his feelings out in ounces like he used to mix his paints. Way back when, I showed him how to let it whoosh the other way, full bore on everything so hard we all got swamped. That's my story, my tale of woe. Whooshed me right to eighteen months in the pokey. Seems like Jesse whooshed himself to eighteen years.

I'm glad he made the hop to Maui. It kind of shook me up, a swerve like that, it goes against his nature. You'd think he'd want to come back to his daily regimen after old home week in Santa Cruz. She's a peach, Natalie, guaranteed to leave you wailing for your momma. Too bad she's such a pill about my money. Her kids need shoes.

Look at Jesse hustle near the visitor's center, stumbling over his laces in the dark, right foot, left foot, as if it doesn't matter how he goes. Keep an eye out for the trailhead, Little Brother, and take care—the weather's cold enough to crack your fillings. Two miles of elevation, the wind jumps through you and your thinking turns to rubber. You might get spooked and lose the trail, lose track of where you are.

Haleakala doesn't pull its punches—the place hands out the big picture whether you want your picture big or not. Those are clouds streaming past your ankles, can't you tell, and the stars, who's ever seen so many, the constellations magnified, Andromeda, Draco, the Northern Crown. Wait till dawn puts out the full show front and center—all that unfiltered ultraviolet, the turbulent geology, the molten center of the earth yanked up so you can crunch your feet on top of it. Like Lucy said, a spot to put you right with God.

They've got a plant there, the only place it grows is in the crater. Silversword, check it out when you get farther down, it's everywhere, a gray-green fuzzy clump, hardly worth a fuss. For fifty years the thing'll sit and mind its quiet business, but come one spring, it grows a stalk head-high or taller. Gorgeous item, thicker than your arm and fluffed crown to root with purple flowers, hundreds of them, some stolen color there amid the desolation. Of course, afterward, the plant survives maybe a month before it withers—bloom and die, just like that. Let's not get too sniffly. At least it blooms.

Jesse shivered while the sunrise cut a yellow line above the crater's lip. He was squeezed into one of Eileen's fleece jackets, and his jeans let the cold in through the ankles. The daylight advanced by degrees—the cinder cones came into shape out of the darkness and the dry plain of the caldera beneath, a whirl of cloud. The wind spun sand across an ocher landscape. After a while, it was possible to think of nothing but the view.

The altitude diminished his troubles, Jesse decided, starved them of oxygen, and as sunrise continued, he circled the Visitor's Center with a lighter spirit than he'd known in days. If he headed back within an hour or so, he could be in Santa Monica by tomorrow's morning prep. The Copain staff would cheer to see him on the job. He walked to the summit and stayed until the sun was fully up, then headed down the main road to where he'd left his car. A circular rainbow dogged him overhead.

Nearby the parking lot, a crush of tourists tested bicycles and heard last-minute instructions from their leader. He was a young guy with shoulder-length blond dreads, and his spiel had the glistening quality of received truth. The road down Haleakala was the world's longest, steepest paved incline, thirty-eight miles of switchbacks and curves. They were minutes from taking the ultra-hairiest fun ride in the world— and best of all, the van had done all the uphill miles. Here was a gig for Marty, Jesse thought. No pain—all gain.

The group wheeled off in ones and twos, the leader at the head. One man hung back. Jesse caught his eye as the guy inspected the pin-tight curves, the long drop that followed, the cloud blanket several hundred yards further on. A T-shirt reading "Ride or Die" expanded over the man's large belly. He was nearly hyperventilating as he churned through the idea of going down. The man was muttering to himself. It sounded to Jesse's ear as a kind of incantation: "Just one sec. Go time, Charles. You've got this. Go, go, go." The whoops of the descending riders faded down the mountainside.

Ride or Die didn't move, however, and set his almost lash-less eyes on Jesse. The poor guy was practically in tears.

Jesse stepped a few yards closer. "I get where you're coming from. It's kind of massive, a ride like this. Lots of ways to fail or fall. So, look—there's no shame in working the problem as hard as you can."

The man smelled of fear, brass in the air. He was doing a ten-count under his breath, his face shuddering with the effort. He held his bike so tightly it was almost bouncing.

Jesse pointed the rider down the road. "On the other hand, you could focus on the glory, on the rush. Once the miles are behind you and you're on the bottom with your friends, put yourself in that. Valhalla time. Fear conquered. You'll all be heroes."

The man licked his lips. The pulsing in his jaw slowed down. He nodded to Jesse and hoisted himself onto his bike. He wobbled down the long incline, scattering pebbles in his wake. "Wait for me, assholes," he cried to the empty road ahead.

Near him a pair of hikers pulled their knapsacks from their trunk. "Beautifully done," the woman said. "I would have bet a dollar that guy was going to quit."

She was seventy or maybe more, a paisley bandanna knotted around her neck. Her blue eyes were bright in the cold, and her white hair was tucked under a ball cap sporting the yin/yang sign. Beside her, a boy opened his bag and checked its contents, counting through a list he'd pulled from his shirt pocket. He looked twelve, Jesse guessed, hiding himself in his chore. The boy was on the small side, and his aviator sunglasses swam on his head. He looked eager, though, happy for the adventure ahead.

Jesse went over to the woman and with her nod, held up her backpack so she could put it on. She grunted with the weight, said thanks. They both looked down the road, Ride or Die a distant speck. "Let's hope my new friend there makes it down the mountain," Jesse said. "Could be I helped him to his doom."

"Well, who can say? But that was a lovely thing to do." She had to halfway shout to be heard above the wind. "I was thinking my grandson and I might want one, too, a pep talk. The walk down and up out of the crater's about eight hours of violence to the knees. We could both handle a little positive motivation."

Jesse considered the request. The woman's legs looked lean and muscled. Her boots were well used, their red laces firmly tied. Her face, what he could see beneath the shadow of her hat, was the picture of determination. As for the boy, he was staring at the trailhead, ready to bolt down the mountain on his own.

"Looks like your grandson can handle anything Haleakala will throw at him. Last thing he needs is a boost from me. As for you, I bet you could carry someone up and down the hill on your back."

She brushed hair off her face and offered him a cocky smile. "You may be right, but I'd never say no to a little white light energy. It does the trick."

"So they say. I've always found it out of reach."

"Ah," the woman said. "We all can find it, though, if we dig deep. For me it helps remember everything is Maya."

Jesse waved his hands at the surroundings. "Even this? The volcano's an illusion?"

The woman tilted up her brim to get a better look at Jesse. "Some scientists think everything's a construct of the mind. Who knows? But it's beautiful up here in the clouds, and ten times more as you continue on. This is my fifth hike down. I drive up now every year since I moved to the island." She pointed to her grandson who was wiggling with impatience. "Kyle here, his first. He's an amazing boy who loves the wild and wooly places. Grandma to the rescue."

"Five times—this must be your spot."

The woman removed her sunglasses to give Jesse a closer look, as if to tell if he were serious or not. "Haleakala's one of the spiritual centers of Mother Earth, you know. They're all over—Sedona, Uluru in Australia, Lake Titicaca in Peru. The one here's less important, but Hawaiians believe it's where the sun god La made light. I come here to pay the god his due. And I'm trying to get something going with Kyle, to challenge him. He's at the age where everything starts to feel stupid."

"So it does. For some of us, that feeling doesn't stop." Jesse looked at his wristwatch. "OK. I've got to get in my car. Tick tock. A pleasure meeting you."

She squared her backpack and flipped her sunglasses on again. "Well then—good times on your journey. Come back here when you don't have to rush."

She raised two fingers to her forehead in salute and headed to the trail, the boy leading the way. A few yards in, she turned toward Jesse. "Have a nice life, OK?" Then she continued along.

Jesse sat in his car as the engine idled. After a minute, he turned it off and grabbed a hat and water bottle and jogged along the trail, scrambling to catch up. When he reached the pair of hikers, they were sharing a canteen. They looked as fresh as when they started, but Jesse was breathing hard. He took off his hat and wiped his face with a sleeve. "You mind some company? I changed my mind."

She smiled. "Well, good for you. Now take my advice and stash that wristwatch in your pocket. This thing's going to take as long as it needs to. But first let's make sure that Kyle is with the program. One man one vote." She tapped her grandson on the shoulder to rouse him from the pop tunes he was bopping to. "This guy wants to walk with us."

Kyle shrugged. "Sure," he said. "Why not?"

They walked on together keeping conversation to a minimum, the woman instructing Jesse to breathe in order through his seven chakras as he hiked. Jesse focused his attention on his feet. One foot in front of another seemed hard enough.

The house was in a state of uproar when Jesse returned to the cabin—Lucy and Eileen had decided this was the day to decorate the baby's room, and furniture lined the hallways. The women were laughing as they struggled with wallpaper and paste. Through the baby's window, the sunset spread its color against the lemon walls.

"What happened to you?" Lucy wanted to know. "We thought you'd fallen into a crater.

But since you're OK, give us a hand. You do know how red your face is, right? Sunblock, man. I should have given you my tube." She handed him a pail of paste. Jesse told them of his day and his companions, the wonders of walking through the crater. Lucy smiled to hear about the hike.

"Sounds like one of those bonus days we get here all the time."

"Guess so," Jesse said. "But, me, I'm back to California as soon as I can find a flight. I've got a business to run and people who depend on me. My real life." Lucy pointed him to the stepladder. "Well, if you're making tracks, go finish the tall spots, OK?"

Dinner featured a papaya salsa, and afterward Jesse organized his belongings. Lucy had taken to the couch with *What to Expect* and she peered over her book while Jesse fetched the box with Marty's ashes from the coffee table. He sank alongside her—seven-and-a-half hours of walking and several more falls had left their mark on his body. "Soon as I land at LAX, I'm calling the masseuse."

"Maybe you'll have a reason to show up again. How are you at washing shitty diapers?"

"I have no idea. But once the baby's here are you sure you and Eileen will want me in your way?"

Lucy sighed. "Is that how you picture yourself, such bad news you better keep your distance? You better let the rest of us in, pal. We're out here waiting." With a grunt, she pushed herself past him and left the room and returned with something she dropped in his lap. A white T-shirt with printing on the front—the Monkey God soaring over a forest, his tail burning, his face a near match to the one Jesse painted long ago on Marty's storefront wall. On the back, in block letters, Hanuman Designs. "I'm blanking," Jesse said. "We did T-shirts from the logo?"

"A friend of mine brought it back from Bali two months ago. A dinky crafts shop in a dinky village up in the mountains. The owner's American, long brown braid, brown eyes, woman who plays salsa music in her store, my friend didn't catch her name. Tell me I'm doing you a favor letting you know."

Jesse took a breath before he examined the image more completely. He could see her hand in it—the bold colors and composition, the fangs upon the creature's face. Isabel had toughened Hanuman up, underlined the heroics. "Her touch has gotten stronger."

Lucy looked at Jesse with curiosity. "Can't say for definite who drew that thing or where or when."

Jesse roughed his fingers over the ink. He recalled the sweep of Isabel's pencil against her drawing paper, the furrow of her brow while she worked. "She'll want to know that Marty died," he said.

"Maybe. Maybe she'll want to know you didn't."

"You have a nicer view of human nature than I do. She lost her house because of me. She had to run away."

"In that case, L.A. calls," Lucy said.

Jesse pushed himself upright. He fought the tremble in his voice. "Keep my distance, you mean?"

He bent down and gave Lucy a kiss and picked up the T-shirt from where it had fallen.

"Thanks for this. I guess I have to learn to know a roadmap when I see one." He grabbed the box with Marty's ashes and went off to finish his packing. He wondered if the women had an atlas. It would be good to check where Bali was.

TWENTY-THREE

J ESSE FOUND NO RECORD OF HANUMAN DESIGNS in the
Bali-wide phone book provided by his bed and breakfast. The name attached itself to all sorts of businesses—
travel agents, restaurants, nightclubs, but Isabel's shop hadn't
made the list. Through his bedroom window, he watched the
fifteen-year-old daughter of the hotel keeper offer up rice
and flowers at a courtyard shrine—for good luck, the guidebooks said, the first breakfast went to the god.

The girl served him breakfast on his veranda while Jesse
tried to focus on his island map. Caustic sunlight blanked
the tiny print—all he could imagine was a long snooze in
the shade and a cold drink when he woke up. The humidity
and temperature had edged a hundred close to dawn. The air
shimmered. Rain coming soon.

His bungalow and three others squared around the family
garden, and he ate his fruit and yogurt among clumps of wild
orchids and scrub palms and the sweetest-smelling hibiscus
he had ever encountered. In front of him, the baby brother
of his waitress chased a gecko through the plants. Jesse called
out to show where the lizard had run, but the boy fled behind
the safety of his sister's hip. She coddled him and whispered
something tender in his ear. Her brown arm was scarred by a
vaccination mark larger than a silver dollar.

"You give the boy a scare." A blond man sitting at the next veranda spoke in a whispery German accent. He was eating rambutan and approached the fruit with knife and fork, paring meat from skin with dexterous attention. More worn than the youthful voice indicated, though; he had the crepey neck of a middle-aged man who'd seen too much sun.

"You may call me Rama," he said. "A name given to me on the first time to Bali. I like it better than Dieter. For this country, it is good to take the name of the divinity."

Jesse introduced himself and at Rama's invitation brought his coffee to the German's table. The children here were scared of Westerners, the man explained, because of movie violence. "White men are the bad guys, and you are so tall. The children learn to be frightened this way. It was not always so."

The door behind Rama opened and they were joined by a barefoot woman in her twenties who wore a bright sarong. She appraised Jesse with the air of someone for whom such surprises were not unusual. Her name was Nicola, Rama said. She spoke a few words in German and took a chair in what there was of sunlight to brush her hair. The stud piercing her left nostril contained a flashing diamond.

Rama asked if pleasure had brought Jesse to Bali and he answered that he was looking for someone. The German sniffed with disapproval. "This is difficult for Bali. Better not to look but to walk and take the beach. At night to visit dances. Who are you thinking to find?" The man looked down his sunglasses toward Jesse in a combination of curiosity and scorn.

"An old friend of my brother's. He asked me to look her up while I was here. Of course, she might not even be on the island. I'm sure you're right and it's a waste of time." Rama's arrogance had drawn the evasion from him—the dodge slid sweetly past his tongue.

"Bravo. Right from the start you are learning."

Rama spoke to Nicola again. She was painting her toenails now and she looked up to laugh, one foot splayed against her chair seat as she applied the polish. In a few paces Rama was at her side and he twisted her foot from its perch with such force she toppled to the ground. She sprang up and cocked her hand into a fist but then marched into the bedroom without taking her payback. Serving it cold, Jesse thought.

The German attempted to shepherd Jesse back to their pleasant breakfast. "You must understand. Niki makes perhaps the greatest insult—on Bali to display the sole of the feet breaks a strong taboo. In some small places one would be beaten badly or driven away. She must pay attention or she will find only trouble."

Jesse parted himself from Rama's grip. "Seems to me she's found it already, Dieter. I see you hurting her again, I'll forget my manners."

"Ah, the American sensibility—Harrison Ford. Do not be concerned for Niki. She is not frightened of true feeling." Rama took a last sip of coffee before following his sweet love inside.

Back on his own veranda Jesse picked up his map. There were hundreds of small towns upcountry; he would start here in the beach district to see if anyone could narrow the field. From the Germans' bedroom rang the sounds of an argument and a slap across skin—whose it was impossible to judge. Jesse ate his yogurt and noted likely villages on his writing pad. Somewhere was the Bali of the guidebooks, the fair tropical isle.

He canvassed as many taxi drivers and merchants as would speak to him about Hanuman Designs. The uniform response was of devoted helpfulness. Everyone nodded excitedly and they caressed the Hanuman T-shirt as though it were a talisman. Yes, they knew the woman and her shop; yes, an American with dark hair; yes, Spanish music. However, everyone was delighted to place her in a different location. The Balinese, it seemed, gave consent out of a sense of charitable obligation—truth bore no part in it. On his second morning, Jesse rented a motor scooter to tour the highlands himself. No wonder Marty had liked it here. Everyone lied as easily as taking a breath.

Tracking down Isabel was simple after Jesse decided her business would center on the fabric arts. He asked at a sewing machine dealer and there it was, her business card—an address in a village near the former royal water palace. In the local custom, the dealer led Jesse softly by the hand and showed him the road to Mount Batur. "President Sukarno vacation there," said the man. "Him spying all day long at the river girls on the gold-plated telescope."

Hanuman Designs was a bungalow built of wood and stucco, and to Jesse's startled eye it bore an eerie resemblance to the cottage in Felton, as if Isabel's life in California had been a rehearsal. The inside was fragrant from freshly dyed cotton. Scores of woven hangings draped the walls and rafters. Their muted colors made Jesse think of the call to prayer.

Isabel sat in the back of the store behind a wooden loom as large as a grand piano. She hummed along with a merengue playing on a boombox, whipping her shuttle through the warp—her whole body rippled as a narrow band of material crept along the threads. Age had rounded her once-sharp cheekbones but her liveliness remained beautifully untouched.

Jesse called her name and waited to see what she would do. She stared at him and shot up from her bench and sat down again and turned off her music. "I heard someone was looking for me. They said tall. I should've guessed."

"I didn't know how else to do this but show up." He wondered if he should squeeze in beside her, then held back, standing awkwardly. "God, you look exactly the same," he told her. "We could be at Lulu's waiting for Jimmy to set up another round of shooters."

She stared at him tight-lipped and unrelenting. The afternoon rains had launched a downpour, and Isabel got up to close her shutters. "It's monsoon, Jesse. Nobody visits Bali now except for druggies and idiots who refuse to believe the travel books. You were never so foolish."

"I came here to see you. I wasn't worried about getting wet."

She said nothing. Some customers entered the store—ten or so well-fed Americans who were equally offended by the weather and Isabel's refusal to bargain. Jesse loved watching how she made them laugh and open their wallets before she shooed the group back toward their tour bus. What a champ she was—put her in a cocktail dress and she could rule front of house at Copain.

Isabel remained behind her sales counter. "You haven't changed either," she said. "Not in any way that matters. Look how you've got your eye on me, as if you know everything there is to know and we've barely said hello. You were always in a big rush, Jesse, but you never really got too far in the end."

"That was me—always waiting for the world to ease my way. Not that it often did. I hope I'm different now."

Isabel held him firmly in her gaze. "I'm not going to wander through old times with you, or anything else you have in mind. Whatever you're planning, I'm not there for it. Not today. Not tomorrow. Not anytime you name."

"Who says I'm planning anything?"

"Because you can't hide it. You want to ask forgiveness for Santa Cruz or you want me to or some horrible combination of the two."

"And if I did? Wouldn't it be good to let that go?"

"Some doors you open at your peril. Haven't you learned that by now? I have." She unfolded a short piece of cloth that was part of her counter display. "This is double ikat weaving, the most painstaking kind I do, each one tells a story. Take it as a keepsake and give me a kiss on the cheek, and then you go home to wherever home is now. If you have any feeling for me that's what you'll do."

Her face lacked a spirit of generosity, Jesse thought, and he left the weaving where it lay. "Marty was killed in a car accident, and I'm not sure it wasn't suicide. For all I know it stretches back all the way to Santa Cruz."

"That changes nothing. I can't let it." Her hands were shaking. "Want me to push you out the door? Because I will."

Age *had* altered her, trimmed away her reliable confidence. Isabel's face was trembling. One or two more words and he could make her cry. If Jesse picked the right ones, maybe she'd let him stay as long as he wanted. They could fix the trouble between them—or not, but they could try. She stood waiting for him, leaning weakly on her counter edge, an inch away from losing her composure.

Jesse drew himself up as tall as he could. "OK. I guess you're right and I should take my leave. I thought we were better friends than this, but I can handle being wrong. I've been making a career out of it lately." He found in his wallet a card from Copain and set it on her counter. "In case you ever change your mind."

Jesse opened the front door and walked outside. The rain slanted at him as though taking aim. In the middle of the road, a pair of mud-soaked dogs tussled over a corncob. They flopped through puddles and howled with unconstrained joy. Jesse stood there blinking away the wet and seeing mostly blur. The dogs chased him out of the village. They were thrilled to do their duty.

The rain had stopped and after a bath and a visit with a travel agent to plan his ticket home, as evening settled, Jesse walked to a shore-side edition of the Hard Rock Café. His last night on Bali and he craved a drink that came with an umbrella and music loud enough to pummel his brain to mush. Of course, hunting down the past had been a fool's errand. He hadn't imagined, though, how it would sting to be the fool.

The restaurant delivered as required—the cheap-jack American culture he normally avoided and a host of beet-red Australians whose purpose seemed to be drinking themselves into a month-long stupor. Pushing through the jouncing bodies, Jesse heard somebody call his name—the German woman, Nicola, who sat by herself at the bar. She motioned him to the empty seat next to her while shouting an order over the counter.

"I'm glad I saw you," she said. "You were brave to take my side with Rama the other morning. I think maybe you frightened him."

"You've been hiding your talents. Your English is first-class."

She accepted his praise with a nod. "Sometimes it's simpler to wear the mask. With Rama's friends, I like to wait and see."

The waiter appeared with their cocktails, and Niki offered a toast to her departed boyfriend. "Rama thinks Bali has been spoiled, too many of the wrong kind of people, too many places like this. He traveled to Lombok to find solitude." She clinked Jesse's glass. "I prefer crowded. Prefer new. Anyhow, the true Bali can be found if you search. Rama's lazy."

"To the wrong kind of people, then. Long may we wave."

Niki's gaze, which in daytime had been forbidding, in the murk of the bar, shone on him benevolently. "Something has hurt you, I think. This was not a brother's friend you were visiting, but a sweetheart. She was not kind to you, I think. I'm sorry, your face shows everything."

Jesse imagined he blushed. "That's what she accused me of. I appear to be an open book." Sunburn colored Niki's throat and he wondered how far down it stretched. "Take me out of here and show me what you love about the island," he said. "The true Bali, whatever turns you on."

They finished their drinks and strolled into the humid evening. "I'm glad we're together," Niki said. She was laughing and she took his hand. "You have an obligation. You came to my defense with Rama. In the old days here, we would be betrothed by now or our families at war."

"Why don't we just start with supper," Jesse said.

They had saté and mushroom omelets from a food stall, Niki watching Jesse clean his plate as though she had a stake in his enjoyment. Their time together would be short and that would make it thrilling, she promised. With the right sequence, they could catch a cockfight *and* a monkey dance and still have time to walk into the rice paddies and hear the frogs and enjoy the fireflies. Her eyes were glittering. "I like this idea extremely—everything at once, as much as possible."

"You'll wear me out."

"I don't think so. I think you can take a lot. Which first, the cockfight or the dance?"

The image of fighting birds gripped the back of Jesse's neck. Cruelty and bloodshed were difficult to jibe with the docile, pleasant-faced Balinese, yet the fights were the national obsession. "Cockfight," he answered.

Niki leaned over the table and kissed him. Apparently, he had passed a test.

They raced their Vespas into the mountains, and Niki barely touched her brakes, the whine of her engine pulling Jesse along the moonlit road faster than he considered possible. He was panting when they finally halted in a small village. Sex with her, if he got that far, was going to be amazing.

The fights were conducted in a courtyard packed with men and were mercifully brief—jagged movement and shouting bettors and bloody feather-down. The handlers fussed over the cocks, breathing life and hope into their beaks as they tightened knife blades to their legs. Jesse found his attention floating above the birds, as though he were watching a formal enactment, something gaudy out of Las Vegas. After two deaths, he was prepared to leave. What could be learned here? The roosters expired with barely a sigh.

Niki's fingers dug into his thigh—they were close to the action and her white T-shirt was faintly spattered with red. It seemed to Jesse the blood stains could be seen as words. The stud in Niki's nostril caught a secret light he couldn't identify, jiggling from silvery to turquoise to ruby, and with every change, a different hum chimed down his spine. Jesse groaned. "Jesus, Niki. What did you do to me?"

Her smile peeled away from her lips. "The mushrooms are coming on already? You must be very sensitive. This is my special surprise—the food stall puts them in your omelet if you ask."

Jesse grunted to his feet and struggled to remember the procedure, fight or flow? Too many years. It was Marty who was maestro of the bummer—talking down a tripper's panic was his stock and trade. Marty was dead.

The crowd pressed in—sweat and kretak cigarettes, the clove smoke everywhere, and Jesse broke to the outermost ring. Niki's voice calling, but how to pluck one note from the chicken-squawk and singsong Balinese? The road, yes, and the red Vespa, the engine barking with a push on the starter. A curve and another, the moon leading him or falling behind, the ride stitched together a single bend at a time. He fell against Isabel's door like a sprinter bursting through the tape. The touch of her fingers. Help me, he said.

I love that about traveling—the random intersection of strangers, the roll of the dice whether today's your day for god or victim, the uncertainty is why you fly six thousand miles. Too bad you couldn't hang in there with Niki, she's a keeper, I can tell. That sleek Euro body, the German thrust of her stare—the kind that used to look ahead a thousand years. OK, her manners need improvement, but I'm sure she meant no harm. Mushrooms fade before you know it, don't they, three or four hours—that's not so long to grit your teeth. And who's to say it wouldn't be all kinds of fun—some pretty pictures, your defenses drizzled away, physics and geometry a matter of conjecture. A little ego death, not the worst thing that could happen. The month you've had, you should have said, "Ooh boy," and kicked back for the ride.

Instead you hiked it home, or the closest version you could find, and lucky for you, Isabel gathered you in. I wasn't sure she would, deep as a dark pool, you saw that for yourself. Besides, what little tenderness the lady has is booked. She'll be your nursemaid for the bye and bye, but futures—it's a bear market, you better take your business elsewhere. Morning's hauling like a freight train, and when it comes, fly back to the home you have for real. Life with Bel's same as with the roosters—strong wins, weak fails, each side born to it.

TWENTY-FOUR

H E SAW THE GIRL AT EARLY LIGHT. She was in her mid-teens and dark like Isabel, her feet planted in the family style—a devotion to the straight-ahead. She scrabbled for something on the dresser. This was her bedroom: the narrow bed Jesse sprawled across, its lavender sheets and the smell of chewing gum on the pillow, the three pairs of flip-flops on the sisal rug. A daughter's room.

He hadn't seen her the night before, while Isabel treated him with orange juice and Xanax and dressed him in batik pajamas, talked him to a soft landing. The night's residue clouded Jesse's calculation—was it within reason that the girl belonged to him? She might be old enough, and her coltish body promised size, though her wide cheekbones and well-shaped nose were more in the Armenian line. She was watching him in her dresser mirror, arranging the scalloped collar of her school uniform, folding it twice before she was satisfied.

He swung his legs over the bed and sat up, clasping his hands on his thighs to conceal the shake. "Hey there. Good morning."

The girl put a finger to her lips. "I'm not supposed to bother you, Mom'll have a fit. I needed my earrings. The old king died in Klungkung and the whole school is going to the funeral. We're supposed to dress up, like you could with these stupid uniforms."

"That doesn't sound like much fun. A funeral."

"Oh, they're really great. All the mourners are in white and there's gamelan, a Barong maybe—that's a kind of puppet lion god. And before the cremation, they spin the body on their shoulders to confuse the soul. That's how it won't find its way back home."

"Is that so bad?"

She rolled her eyes. "Ghosts make mischief and they love revenge. Everybody knows."

"Fascinating," Jesse said. "I'd like to hear more about it when you have a chance. If you tell me your name, I can ask you nicely."

"Aster. And you're Jesse. You were Mom's friend a long time ago."

"When I met her, I wasn't too much older than you."

Her face softened—the look he guessed she saved for holy men and beggars. "Mom said you're going away before I get home from school."

"I don't know. I may loiter around the house."

"Like a ghost?" The girl had a musical laugh. "No offense."

"None taken," Jesse said. He watched from his window as she left for school. Aster Lantana. Two flowers.

Jesse went hunting for Isabel. He shuffled from room to room, glancing at the few pieces of furniture and nosing into the kitchen cabinets and tiny refrigerator. For a while, he stood in the center of the living room to see if he could parse the life that passed between its walls. Whatever he looked at, picture frame, footstool, his own pajamas, for that matter, was made by hand and with the Balinese impulse for color and design. A stylish life but one of modest requirements. If Isabel was happy, it was in a minor key.

He found her doing yoga in the courtyard between house and shop, moving briskly through the asanas. Her body was as sturdy as he remembered, her features sun-bright and stripped of feeling. Overhead, wild parrots roosted in the bougainvillea. The beating of their wings blended with the stroke of Isabel's breath.

She adopted a lying-down posture he recalled as Lord Vishnu's Couch, and Jesse set himself atop the cobblestones to follow along, forcing the leg extension with painful effort. Isabel sighed as he struggled to achieve the pose. "You can't hop in like that, you'll hurt yourself." Annoyance colored her voice, yet Jesse imagined there was tenderness, too.

"I'm not hoping for nirvana, just a little wake-me-up," he said. Isabel carried on without waiting to see how he managed.

After they were done, she showered and brought out breakfast and asked him how he was feeling. "You put the fear of God in me last night. The mushrooms had you babbling about the soles of your feet and setting the forest on fire with your tail."

Jesse extended an almost-steady arm to show his level of repair. "I'm on the mend, thanks to your good graces and the contents of your medicine chest. You always had that nurse's touch." An impatient smile forced itself onto Isabel's face. "Liar."

While they ate, Jesse told a little of his years in Santa Monica, describing Copain's success and his catastrophe of a marriage. "I can handle Helena as a business partner, but as a wife, call out the National Guard. Nowadays, I point her toward the competition and say, 'Kill.' Better them than me." Isabel drank her tea in silence.

He went on with what he knew of Marty's recent life. There was no way to shape the story or blunt the blow of his death on Route 11. The telling poured out of him as Jesse pictured for her the Somerville apartment, its books and mildewed quilt and $40 bourbon, then Lieb and his paintings and cigars, the InfoCon bequest. The ironies were merciless and plentiful, but none of them brought Isabel to tears.

"It sounds like Marty's bad habits finally caught up with him," she said when Jesse's stories had run out.

"Maybe he just lost his way. If I hadn't turned him in..."

"If. You did what you saw necessary. Same as everybody does, Marty certainly, every chance he got."

She seemed so sure of her ground, it put her at a remove that Jesse didn't know how to close. "I wanted better of myself," he said.

Isabel stood. Sunlight washed over her, bright flecks shining in her hair as though she were lit from within. "We all do. Thank heaven nobody's keeping score."

Jesse felt a wave of sadness wash through his chest. "I am. I always have."

"But you can stop. Just stop. It took me years to figure that out for myself. Give yourself a break and see how it feels."

With a nod of adjournment, she piled up the breakfast dishes and straightened the table.

"I'd like to think I made a hit with Aster this morning." Jesse fought to shade a note of lightness to his tone. "Would you mind if I stayed for dinner and had a real goodbye?"

Isabel measured him with a stare. "As long as that's all it is and you leave afterward."

"Don't worry. I've been making exits all month. I've got it down." He watched her go off to open her shop for customers. The rattle of the loom filled the still, hot courtyard.

After dinner there was algebra, and Aster demanded Jesse's attendance. He sat on her bed as she pondered word problems at her desk, talking herself through the steps, finding the equations buried within stories about bus trips, cookie sales, and party invitations. Aster clapped her hands and cheered herself on with every happy success. She was Marty's kid—it was broadcast in everything she did. The world was made for girls like her.

At one point Aster looked up from her notebook. "Did you know my dad?" She spoke casually, and at first Jesse thought the girl was repeating something from her text. Various answers dried in his mouth. "No," he said carefully. "What was his name?"

Aster was doodling on her page, curlicues and flowers and a pretty cabin on a hill. "Carlo, Mom said. He was Italian, a tourist, I guess. But he died before I was born. He drowned body-surfing in Nusa Penida—she won't show me where."

"Do you think it would make a difference if you knew?"

Aster put down her pencil. "I think she's mean. I don't know anything real." Her yearning touched him, the wounded dampness in her young eyes.

"Only in math books does the world line itself up in columns."

"I don't like it. It's unfair."

"So it is," Jesse said.

They said their goodbyes when her homework was finished, Aster kissing his cheek shyly. He closed her door and heard her talking to herself. Double-checking her math results before she went to bed.

Her mother sat at a courtyard table beneath a string of paper lanterns. The place before her was scattered with loose snapshots and an open photo album, and she was drinking Johnny Walker from a water glass, small, ladylike sips as she pasted pictures in her book. "Hear those frogs? When I moved here, the night sounds made me crazy, I barely slept. Frogs and dogs. Dogs and frogs."

Jesse took the chair next to her. "You got used to it, though."

"I got used to it. I learned to be light on my toes. My tippy-toes. Of course after a bit I had my baby. With a child you switch to hunker down."

"You've done an amazing job. She's quite the girl. Dancing forward and the universe be damned. Just like Marty."

A long silence fell between them. Beyond the courtyard, fireflies darted above the garden: motion upon motion and a pale green glow, and all for love. Isabel, however, was watching Jesse with a sadness familiar to him—a plea for ending things without more words.

Jesse picked up her glass and drank the whiskey down. "I'm guessing Marty never knew about Aster. And she has Carlo. More tragic than the real story, but now only a few millimeters shy of what really happened. Maybe one day you'll be able to tell her the truth."

Isabel's jaw quivered, but Jesse pressed on. "OK, the past stays where it is—you have your reasons. But the future, Bel, let me help you with the future. Marty left a large estate. You and Aster could return home, buy a house in Felton or anywhere. Money for college and beyond. The man would be doing cartwheels. He never had the chance to make amends."

Isabel poured herself another whiskey. "There are no amends."

"Sure there are. Marty left a trail of disaster a mile wide and a decade long."

Isabel leaned forward and fluffed her fingertips through the curls at Jesse's temples and touched his cheek. "Look at you, gray as a grandpa. And me, I'm nothing but spots and wrinkles, a million marks of age and failure. I've given up looking into mirrors, I leave that for Aster. But you, you're desperate to pick over everything we are and were, and there'll be no blinking and nothing left out. You want the mirror head on. OK. I'm tired of fighting you off."

A breeze jostled the overhead fixtures, and in the dancing light, Isabel seemed to have lost her substance, as though she was floating above her chair. The imprint of her fingers still warmed Jesse's skin. She leaned forward so that the wind wouldn't chop into her words. "There are no amends because Marty did nothing, was responsible for nothing, was let in on nothing. The blue jeans deal was mine not his. My own secret arrangement through people I knew from my Hollywood days. I was planning to bring everybody into it, you included, but only after the fact, for safety's sake. But then you got arrested and everything exploded."

"I don't believe you," Jesse said. "Why would Marty go through eighteen months in jail for something he didn't do?"

"For me," Isabel said with little enthusiasm. "To play the gentleman for once. To be the big man. Of course, I skipped off quickly enough, anyway. Finding my lifeline, first and always."

"While Marty and I were free-falling?"

Isabel sat with her hands in her lap. "Yes. I had to. I'm sorry."

It took Jesse a moment to find his voice. "I once imagined you were the answer to all my problems. It's a hard habit to break and I'm sure it got in your way, how I tried to love you. But I never lied to you, not that I remember. Not once."

Isabel looked at him. Her dark eyes were damp. "No. The only one you lied to was yourself."

Jesse rose to his feet. "Marty's lawyer will be calling. The name is Lieb. Don't let him hand you the runaround."

Isabel tilted her face toward Jesse. "Please, I don't want anything."

"It's not for you." He thought he could kiss her goodbye, but Isabel had picked up a snapshot of herself and Aster—the two of them in bathing suits, the girl clinging to her mother's back as they jumped into a river. There was a looseness in Isabel's photo smile that rendered her unfamiliar, caught as she was between what she knew and what she didn't. Water spray misted mother and daughter from head to toe. You couldn't tell where one ended and the other began.

TWENTY-FIVE

CONFESSION LANCES THE SPIRIT, so the padres tell us, and the shrinks, and I can think of more than once I tried to phone you up to own my history as Isabel's champion and patsy. Something always held me back, Jesse. Worry for the lady's well-being, not that she deserved it, not that I knew where she was, and a need for peace and quiet. Middle age had cured me of my craving for commotion. Vanity, of course, was still my number one—the swollen image of myself I'd lugged around since I was out of diapers. No way I wanted you to know me as I was: a faithful lapdog sold out by somebody I trusted.

And so I gave you the role as the aggrieved, and I played mine as your betrayer. I missed your wedding, your restaurant success, and your divorce. You missed my slow approach on wealth, my simultaneous decline. Funny how that works. The shinier my balance sheet, the more I had to spend my time alone—stung once, I guess, forever shy. The "yo" I grunted at the toll-booth gal the night I drove to Lincoln was the first I'd said to anyone in days.

Did we ever make that trip together, I can't remember. Country roads in midwinter, the Milky Way above the ridge near Lafayette, so much twirling energy and stellar dust and light, the whole cosmic do-si-do. Once or twice a season I hit the White Mountains in my junker hunting for vistas. Christ, the overflow of space in three dimensions made me happy, slammed my point of view into proportion, shrank me down to size. How could I resist, I floored the gas until it felt like I was zooming through those stars myself—the farthest thing from suicide there is.

I never saw the deer who jumped into my headlights, a twelve-point buck, according to the local news, plenty big to dent my belly and throw my car into the rail. We built ourselves a handsome pile of litter, didn't we, skid marks and crushed iron, animal blood spoiling that double white line. I always could be counted on to leave my mess for someone else to tidy up. That's you, Jesse. Now and always.

What made you go those miles from Somerville to Bali, spreading my little tale to anyone who'd care? Guilt, was it, or loyalty to what our time in Santa Cruz had been, or love? Nothing to be ashamed of, love, it starts wars and builds cathedrals, why can't it spur you to a little trip? Wasn't it love that got you to lay the money on the kid, even if it makes her mommy squirm? I say send them every dime and let the future roll.

She's got moves already, Aster, hasn't she, soul as wide as the world and a mind that skips around corners, Isabel's gypsy looks. We'll have to pray she makes it through without her daddy's touch but all his nature. Maybe you'll check in on her from time to time. Maybe you shouldn't. Maybe you can't.

Enjoy your peace and quiet, you've earned it ten times over—that long hike from Isabel's gave you too much time to think. So go ahead and hole up on that beach till you turn baby pink, watch the local women scrounge for shells—they step so neatly, look, they never get their clothing wet. They don't like the sea, the Balinese, it scares them, evil spirits, and they keep their distance. But we can't get enough, the air the flavor of the womb, the light dimpling off the water, so many kinds of blue you lose count. It thumps the heart to see the breakers crash on shore without even a tiny intermission, some of them higher than your waist, some small and feather-light. It's the teeny ones that make the sand, Jesse, crumbling rock until it shines like diamonds. All it takes is patience.

The airport taxi was due, but Jesse didn't mind making it wait. Every so often he could swivel under his beach umbrella and spy his landlord standing where the hotel path reached the sand, the fellow poised with one hand on the knot of his sarong while the foolish American in his black bikini underwear refused to come out to meet his obligation. In the Balinese way, the man was too polite to step forward and raise a fuss.

Jesse had worn away the early hours at a travel office arranging his afternoon flight to Los Angeles. Humble pie and bluster had been the order of the morning, and it had pleased him to roll out the full battery of his persuasive skills to pry loose a ticket on a sold-out plane. But as time passed and the metallic sunlight bore down and the sea breeze tickled his hair, the thought of hurrying home seemed a mistake like everything else he'd done since leaving Somerville the month before. Pick your lifeline and let everyone else fall in behind— so had gone Isabel's instruction. How on earth was it applied?

Noon was approaching, and the beach glowed white, yet all around him, sunbathers soaked up the ultraviolet. Jesse was convinced he spotted Rama and Niki sleeping on a nearby blanket, their limbs carelessly entwined. Love endured in its fashion. There was a lesson there, too.

He picked up the cardboard box that sat beside him and carried it to the shoreline. Marty's ashes. It was heavier than ever and bruised from travel, the green color faded; it looked like it had been to the moon. The waves lined up for their next set. Jesse fixed on his goggles and dove beneath the first breaker.

He was pounded five feet down where the water was cool and glassy and graced by filtered light and darting fish. With a sharp tug to the lid, the box exploded in a cloud of silvery ash and bone. Glitter streamed in the current. Jesse watched it eddy and fall. And then the pressure in his chest pushed him gasping to the surface.

Amazing, he was gritty with the stuff, streaks on his shoulders and face and coating his goggles, the flint of it on his lips. Marty, true to form down to the very end, demanding the final word.

A wave shaped up behind him. Jesse swam to meet it and put himself in its care. He rode to shore laughing with all the strength in his body. He was naked but he didn't know it.

ACKNOWLEDGMENTS

Thanks to the many hands whose fingerprints are all over this manuscript. First to Andre Dubus II. You showed me the way. To my current and former workshop members. Your patience, careful reading, and good humor kept me on track during this book's long development. Lori Ambacher, Cindy Anderson, Louie Cronin, Claudia Franklin, Judy McAmis, Peter Orner, Adair Rowland, Bob Steinberg, Jep Streit, and Frankie Wright—I love you guys.

Thanks to David Talbot. Your enthusiasm and brilliant advice gave me a much-needed late boost.

Special thanks to Ruth Henrich and Bonnie Mettler for editing and design. Your work makes mine look like the real thing. And thank you, Alex Deidda of www.aledesign.co.uk for my beautiful website.

Thanks to the members of the ALLi Facebook group. You answered my ongoing questions with more forbearance than I deserved.

To my parents, Iver and Bernice, who started me as a reader. You were there in bed, books in hand, night after night. And especially to my mom, who passed onto me her love of writing. To my brother, Dan, who left behind lists of books he'd finished and ones he wanted to get to next. To my Canton family, Bidu, Rac, Zander, and Zella—none of this would be fun without you.

And last and most of all, to Carol, whose energy, determination, and love prove daily what an artist's life can be. We said "forever," and I guess we meant it.

 RICHARD RAVIN has written for the *San Francisco Examiner, Salon.com, The Daily News of Newburyport*, and was anthologized in *Andre Dubus: Tributes*, Xavier Review Press. Before turning to writing fiction, he worked as a production executive in Hollywood, overseeing the creation of more than forty television movies and miniseries. He lives in Massachusetts. He is currently at work on his second novel, a detective story.

You can find him at www.richardmravin.com

CPSIA information can be obtained
at www.ICGtesting.com
Printed in the USA
LVHW031613290121
677805LV00004B/174